THE
ARMAGEDDON GAME

by

Lynne Fox

For John Fisher whose support and
encouragement never wanes.

Thank you.

ACKNOWLEDGEMENTS

My thanks must go to John Fisher for his helpful comments on the first draft. Also to Kevin Saunders for his erudite suggestions and for pointing out a glaring error!

The cottage stood alone against the barren landscape of the headland, with its back to the sea as protection against the worst of the weather it made a defiant stand against the crashing violence of the waves.

The only approach was a single track covered with a thick layer of snow and ice that crackled under Inspector Munroe's tyres and hid the ruts and potholes. He drove with extreme caution, the journey a nerve-wracking test of his vehicle's suspension.

Pulling up outside the front door, once painted a jaunty maritime blue but now peeling in layers, he stepped out of the car. His feet sank into the soft snow just deep enough that it topped the rim of his shoes, the warmth from his body melting it on contact. His woollen socks soaked up the moisture, the cold travelling up his legs at an alarming rate. He shuddered, shoved his hands into his jacket pockets and hunching down against the arctic atmosphere, trudged toward the cottage door.

The police tape had long since been removed, the only evidence of its ever being there a couple of short lengths still tied to the chicken wire fencing, flapping like ticker tape in the wind. The door was unlocked, forensic had gathered all its evidence months ago and the place was no longer of interest as a scene of crime.

Turning the round knob handle he pushed against the door's resistance. The damp salt air had warped both door and frame so that he had to place his shoulder against it and use his full body weight to force it. Opening with a reluctant, ear-piercing shriek as it scraped over the wooden floor it was as though the cottage itself resented his intrusion.

Pushing it shut he stood with his back to the door, his eyes slowly adjusting to the gloom within. His breath hung in the air, frosted crystals of moisture; it seemed colder in here than outside. Instinctively he gathered his jacket closer to him as though huddling into a cosy duvet although it did nothing to dispel the cold. Nothing moved; the air inside the cottage was as still as the air inside a sepulchre, fetid with the lingering sweet smell of rotting flesh.

Outside the clouds briefly parted allowing the sun's rays to pierce the grime on the window to his right sending a shaft of brilliance across the room. Like a macabre stage setting it illuminated a deep seated armchair.

With effort he took a couple of steps forward feeling he was dragging his legs through molasses; his eyes darting about the room as though expecting someone to be there.

Beginning in the far left corner he slowly and methodically canvassed every piece of furniture, every cloth covering. He pulled books from the bookshelf, opening each one and shaking them in turn. Idly he fingered a couple of the chess pieces, still laid out on the table, wondering if there was some significance in their positions on the board but he'd never played the game so its nuances meant little to him. Taking hold of one of the two wooden dining chairs he climbed onto it to give him more height and ran his fingers along the picture rail. What he was looking for he didn't rightly know. The forensic team had gone over the scene with meticulous care; he didn't doubt their diligence or expertise but there had to be something; something they had missed and he would stay here, searching, until he found it.

Three hours later, each of the four rooms examined and still nothing. He'd completely lost track of time, even the gradual fading of light hadn't registered; he'd simply taken out his torch to examine things more closely. Now, as he looked out the window he realised there was no way he would be driving back tonight. The snow had increased to a blizzard whilst he was inside; now covering the earth like an animal *pelt. It was a complete white-out, the screaming gale and ferocious crashing of the waves below him a disembodied voice of a soul in torment.*

As he stood by the kitchen window his hand knocked against a kerosene lamp standing on the draining board. He lifted it cautiously and felt the weight and heard the slosh of its liquid fuel. Fumbling in his pocket he found his lighter and with a misplaced sense of relief, lit the mantle.

CHAPTER 1

It's been three years since I was returned to St Joseph's Psychiatric Hospital, the past two spent in the wing for the criminally insane because I'd killed Dr Metcalfe during one of our therapy sessions.

The authorities were none too pleased with me. Dr Metcalfe had been the hospital's shining light, an advocate for adopting more humane treatment of the psychologically deranged. The general consensus had been that I was evidence such an approach was flawed so security had been enhanced, rules more stringently followed and any outside interference with the running of St Joseph's strongly opposed.

There were no strait jackets or inmates manacled to beds and to my knowledge the one and only padded cell had never been used. It was more a case of constant surveillance. The security cameras had been increased three-fold and no-one from my wing ever went anywhere without a minder, two in the case of the more unpredictable.

I was now down to one having behaved myself impeccably since the Dr Metcalfe incident and he – his name was Alberto – was becoming more relaxed in my company. I'd never told why I'd killed Dr Metcalfe; there was little point as I knew they'd never believe me so I said nothing.

My new therapist, Dr Chang, brought all his many years of experience and knowledge to bear but still was unable to elicit my reason. He didn't have the calm, self-assurance of Dr Metcalfe; his frustration was palpable. Quite a non-descript little Chinese man he wore suits made of a pale yellowish beige that his skin colour merged with so well that, in half light, it was difficult to determine where Dr Chang left off and the suit began.

Of course, Dr Chang's therapy sessions and the many pills I obediently swallowed weren't going to cure me because I wasn't criminally or otherwise insane. I'd known exactly what I was doing, I always have. In the case of Dr Metcalfe it was clear, after what he'd told me, that whilst he was in control of St Joseph's I would never be discharged so killing him didn't exactly alter my situation.

Of course, the wing I was now on was somewhat more austere than the rest of the hospital but it was liveable with. The bed was comfortable enough even if the mattress was made of a material that resisted heat, ripping or tearing and the base made of extremely tough moulded glass fibre. My room was sparse but there were a few hooks for hanging things albeit made of moulded rubber so they bent over if any real weight was put on them and the clothes hangers were of cardboard. Bars on the windows and observation slits in the door were no different to the general wards so I was used to that.

The only real downside was the layout of the building. St Joseph's was Victorian and built on a radial plan with long wings stretching out from a central hub. The majority of these wings had been demolished to make way for better design but the criminally insane were still housed in those that remained. This design led to a lack of natural light and prevented a healthy circulation of air and is generally regarded these days as inhumane but I guess the trustees of St Joseph's felt it was all we deserved, However, there were compensations; we were still allowed to use the gym and swimming pool, had Sky TV and plenty of recreational activities.

Of course, to have any of these benefits one had to show willing and take part in the various therapy sessions; both the one to one's with an allotted therapist and the group sessions. I enjoyed the group sessions best; it was fascinating to listen to the other inmates baring their souls, displaying their vulnerabilities – an excellent finishing school for a psychopath!

All in all, being in St Joseph's again wasn't so bad but I had no intention of remaining in the care of the psychiatric profession any longer than I had to; how to get out was the problem. The first step was to be moved back into the lesser risk accommodation and in that respect I was well on the way to persuading Dr Chang that I no longer posed any threat; that Dr Metcalfe was simply an aberration; I knew I'd been a naughty girl and I'd never do it again.

I'd just finished a session with Dr Chang and could sense he was close to transferring me when we were interrupted by one of the nurses. She walked across and whispered in Dr Chang's ear, giving surreptitious glances in my direction as she did so. He made a brief nod of acknowledgement and turned to me as the nurse quietly closed the door behind her.

'Annalee, there's an Inspector Munroe at reception asking to speak with you. He apparently has some news for you regarding your parents. Will you meet with him?'

Possibilities raced across my mind; death, accident, divorce? Did I really care one way or the other? I hadn't seen them for years; they'd emigrated to Australia during my first sojourn in St Joseph's. Yet it would be interesting to see how Inspector Munroe was faring; he and I went back a long way and he, along with Dr Metcalfe, was primarily the reason I was back in St Joseph's. I gave a slightly concerned look toward Dr Chang. 'Will you be with me?'

'No, but Alberto will be.' Dr Chang looked across at Alberto, sitting mute in the back of the room; since Dr Metcalfe no-one except Alberto was inclined to be alone with me.

I turned toward him also. 'Oh, ok then,' and smiled warmly.

Alberto was a tall, black man, extremely handsome with the physique of a prize fighter. I could never understand why he had been appointed my main supervisor; with his attributes I would have thought he'd be far more useful with one of the burly, violent inmates. Despite Dr Metcalfe I was hardly a physical threat; female, diminutive – only five foot three – he could restrain me with one hand. Still, he *was* gorgeous and although I wouldn't claim we'd formed a friendship we did have a mutual respect aided by the fact that I was secretly helping him with his written English.

'The Inspector has been shown to Room 1-4-5, Alberto.' Dr Chang closed his copious file on me with, I felt, a sense of relief and Alberto ushered me from the room.

DCI Munroe rose from the chair on which he was sitting, good manners obviously deeply ingrained then, remembering who it was he was standing to greet, swiftly sat down again retracting his proffered hand. 'Miss Theakston.'

It was clear his animosity toward me had not lessened with the passing of time. He continued to believe that I was responsible for the death of his daughter, Lily. His turning up again so unexpectedly was a little disconcerting. As far as I was concerned the game was over; with the death of his daughter I'd had my revenge for what I considered was his part in the death of my brother yet I had to admit that I'd missed our verbal confrontations; the intellectual challenge had been stimulating. Sparring with the doctors in St Joseph's was dull by comparison.

'Good morning, Inspector, it's been a long time; I trust you are well.'

I could tell, with some satisfaction, that he was anything but well. He had always been, to my mind, painfully thin but now he was almost skeletal. He'd lost more of his hair, the bald patch at the crown being crept up upon by the widow's peak rapidly forming at the front; his cheeks were sunken with darkness about the eyes and his overly long neck poked out from a slightly loose shirt collar, sinewy tendons clearly visible. As he crossed his legs his trousers flapped about them like a skirt there was so much unrequired material. It was obvious the years had not been kind to Inspector Munroe.

Alberto directed me to the upright chair opposite Munroe then retired to the side of the room and leant against the wall. Munroe's eyes drifted over toward him.

'Alberto is my minder,' I explained, 'he goes with me everywhere.' I smiled sweetly.

Munroe cleared his throat. 'Miss Theakston, I have some news regarding your parents.'

'So I've been given to understand.'

'You may not have been aware but at the time of your trial and conviction for the murder of Dr Metcalfe's fiancée, Melissa Hartnell …'

I raised my hand to stop him. 'Which I *did not commit*.'

Munroe took a deep breath and continued, ignoring my interruption. '… the authorities advised your parents, as next of kin, of events.'

'How very considerate.'

Refusing to be distracted Munroe ploughed on. 'They expressed a wish to be kept informed of your progress and treatment although they have continued to refuse any direct contact with you.'

I said nothing, gazing at Munroe impassively. I could tell he was warming to his subject. His eyes glittered slightly in the finger of sunshine that was creeping across the room.

'So, when your circumstances changed …'

I raised an incredulous eyebrow. 'Please, Inspector there's no need to be coy, you mean when I killed Dr Metcalfe.'

'Just so, Miss Theakston, when you killed Dr Metcalfe I naturally took steps to inform your parents but not getting any response I contacted my counterparts in Australia.' Munroe shifted slightly in his seat, uncrossing his legs and leaning forward toward me, his elbows on his thighs. 'I'm sorry to tell you, Miss Theakston that your mother has died in suspicious circumstances and your father has confessed to killing her.' Obviously anything but sorry Munroe couldn't resist adding, very quietly as though to himself, 'seems to run in the family, doesn't it?'

Refusing to rise to the bait I merely asked, 'What has any of this got to do with me?'

Munroe, affronted at my lack of concern said, 'They are your parents, I would have thought you would at least be interested in how any of this has come about; what the Australian police have discovered.'

'Very well, Inspector please, enlighten me.'

'I believe you are aware that both your parents have an issue with alcohol.'

I snorted derisively. 'Oh please, Inspector do drop the niceties. They were both functioning alcoholics.'

'Indeed, so I understand. It seems that during one of their alcohol-fuelled arguments your mother confessed to an affair thirty two years ago that resulted in a pregnancy. The child she consequently bore was you. Miss Theakston, I'm sorry to have to advise you that you are *not* your father's biological child. When he learnt of your mother's deception – one that had continued for the vast majority of their marriage – Mr Theakston confessed that he completely snapped and helped on by his alcohol-induced state dealt your mother a blow which resulted in her death.'

Munroe leant back in his chair and re-crossed his legs, barely able to keep the satisfied smirk from his face and recalling our previous encounters continued. 'It seems that you needn't have bothered with the personas you adopted in the past when playing your little games – you're not who you thought you were anyway – quite ironic, don't you think?'

The smugness in his tone was infuriating. I tucked my hands under my legs, sitting on them to control the anger that was bubbling up inside, forcing myself into a display of outward calm. 'Well, thank you for that, Inspector. What happens now?'

'As your father, I beg your pardon Mr Theakston has confessed there won't be much of a trial, more a matter of sentencing. I'll keep you informed of what the judges decide.'

'Thank you, that's very kind.' I stood indicating the meeting was at an end. Alberto levered himself off the wall and came towards me. 'Just a thought, Inspector; did my mother divulge *who* she had her affair with?'

'According to Mr Theakston, no, only that it was someone associated with the firm where she worked all those years ago.'

'I see.' I turned away but as an afterthought paused at the door, 'I almost forgot to ask, so rude of me; how is Mrs Munroe?'

Munroe stiffened, hesitated and turned away before he spoke. 'Mrs Munroe is as well as can be expected.'

'Oh dear, I'm *so* sorry; I imagine it's the death of your daughter, Lily? I would think that would put an intolerable strain on anyone. How are you bearing up?'

Munroe said nothing, merely stared at me, the hatred in his eyes unmistakable.

'Good day, Inspector. I'll wait to hear of developments.' With that I glanced at Alberto and walked out of the room.

CHAPTER 2

Sitting by the barred window back in my room I pondered the news DCI Munroe had given me. It was moments like this that I really missed Liliad, my marionette. For many years she'd been a constant companion, someone I could bounce ideas off. I know she didn't talk back, I'm not insane but somehow talking to her made things clearer; she was my silent support, the only one I was ever truly myself with.

I'd bought her several years previously from a toy shop in The Lanes in Brighton. Normally I'd walk past a toy shop window without giving it a second glance but something, I was never quite sure what, had drawn me to the layout. My eyes scanned the various items; plastic trains, skipping ropes, Lego, jigsaws, picture books – the whole paraphernalia of children's entertainment but nothing captured my attention and I was about to turn away when my gaze was inexorably drawn toward the back of the display.

A doll stared back at me, her wide blemish-free oval eyes compelling me to remain. Her irises were as green as ivy with huge pupils the deep liquid black of its berries. I felt as though I was falling. Transfixed by the delicacy of her features, the craftsmanship was so exquisite I thought she was made of porcelain.

Without conscious thought I found myself inside the shop. The owner, his hands fluttering before him like an agitated butterfly, was instantly by my side. 'I see you've noticed our marionette,' he observed.

'Marionette? I thought it was just an ordinary doll.'

'Oh dear me no; there's nothing 'ordinary' about this little lady.' So saying he reached across and extracted her from amongst the other toys. Up close my eyes widened in further surprise. 'She's made of wood!'

'Indeed, what did you think she was made of?'

'Well, she's so delicate I thought it was porcelain or something.'

He smiled knowingly. 'An understandable mistake; in fact she's carved from a solid piece taken from the centre of an ancient oak. If you look closely at her torso …' he gently pulled up the little blouse, '… you can see the rings of the tree growth. She is the heart of the oak and it continues to live through her.'

Untangling the strings he held her a few inches above the ground. 'Here, you take hold and see if you can make her move.'

Gently he placed my fingers in the correct positions, 'Make her walk toward the door.'

To my delight she strode forward.

'You're a natural,' he exclaimed.

'It's so easy; I don't feel I'm doing anything much.'

His smile widened but he said nothing, just waited.

'How much?' I asked and she was mine.

They'd taken her away from me after the Dr Metcalfe incident, concerned that I might strangle myself with her strings or tear off a wooden limb to fashion a weapon. Complete nonsense as I had no intention of killing myself and would never deliberately hurt Liliad for any reason. For the present Liliad is confined to a shelf in the locked store room. Lately, in return for his English lessons I've managed to persuade Alberto to take me down there and let me have a few private moments with her. She's taking her incarceration with a stoicism that makes me proud, believing unerringly that we will be together again one day. I do not intend to disappoint her.

I closed my eyes to more precisely recall my meeting with DCI Munroe. I wasn't surprised at his ill-concealed pleasure at the news he had to impart; in his eyes he had good reason to hate me. He believed that I had killed his daughter, Lily. She had fallen while on a hiking trip in Scotland and all Munroe had was a photograph that she'd instinctively clicked as she'd gone over the edge which showed a small section of someone's sleeve but the image was so blurred it was impossible to pick out any distinguishing features.

Despite all his efforts Munroe had been unable to prove my involvement and instead had me convicted for the murder of Dr Metcalfe's fiancée, Melissa Hartnell. It was true I'd deliberately befriended her and had enjoyed myself creating a sense of distrust between her and Dr Metcalfe aiming to ruin their relationship but to convict me of killing her had been a complete fabrication based on purely circumstantial evidence as the irony was I really hadn't killed *her*.

Seeing him again after so long was a welcome break from the monotony of St Joseph's; I'd run rings around him in the past yet I had to acknowledge he'd won the last confrontation; after all, I was back in St Joseph's and that was a major problem.

◆

It was a couple of months later that Inspector Munroe turned up again. By now I was out of the high security wing having been correct in my assessment that Dr Chang considered me no longer a risk.

They'd allowed me to keep Alberto as my main carer; the nurse who'd held that position on my previous stay, Betty Fletcher apparently refusing to have anything more to do with me; understandable I suppose, I'd always thought she had a soft spot for Dr Metcalfe. The current situation suited me fine, Alberto was far more malleable and definitely better looking.

Once again in room 1-4-5 I observed Munroe with amusement; he seemed to be torn between a sadistic pleasure at the news he was about to impart and an opposing desire not to have anything to do with me.

'Miss Theakston, I'm afraid I have to be the bearer of more upsetting news,' he paused, obviously relishing the moment, 'your father, or rather, Mr Theakston ...'

'You may continue to refer to him as my father, Inspector, after all he and I both believed he was for over thirty years. It seems churlish to deny him that title now.'

Munroe shrugged, 'Very well, as you wish. I'm sorry to have to tell you that your father hung himself whilst in prison awaiting trial.'

I didn't react to Munroe's news although I did feel a slight disappointment in my father; to give up so soon seemed like a betrayal of self. 'Is that all, Inspector?'

Munroe hesitated, unsettled by my lack of concern. 'Yes, I suppose it is except that I'm informed by the Australian police that the solicitors dealing with your father's estate will be in touch with you shortly. They've been passed your current address.'

'I see, I shall wait to hear then.' I stood giving a beckoning glance to Alberto who moved to open the door but as a parting shot I said to Munroe, 'I wonder if we will meet again, Inspector.'

Munroe spoke as though the prospect was his worst nightmare. 'I sincerely hope not, Miss Theakston, I see no reason why our paths should cross in the future.'

I simply smiled and left the room.

Turning to Alberto as we made our way back to the main lounge I asked, 'Alberto, do you think Dr Chang will let me have Liliad back again now that I'm so greatly improved? Would you ask him please?'

Alberto nodded.

'Thank you I won't forget your help.' I glanced at the lounge clock, 'Oh good, it's almost lunchtime.'

Alberto was as good as his word, or in his case his silent nod; Liliad was back! I can't express what a joyful reunion it was. She was a little grimy from all her months sat on a shelf in the store cupboard but I cleaned her with meticulous care until her black hair gleamed like spilled oil and her eyes sparkled with a renewed mischief.

I was just bringing her up to date with Munroe's latest revelation when Alberto walked in bearing an airmail letter. Normally any correspondence for inmates would have been opened by the hospital authorities but as Alberto had been present at my meetings with Inspector Munroe and so was aware of the circumstances I'd managed to persuade him that in this instance it would not only be inappropriate for the trustees of St Joseph's to be made aware of my dealings with the Australian solicitors but such communications should rightly be kept private. Also, coming as it did from a reputable firm of solicitors it was hardly likely to contain anything untoward.

Consequently Alberto made it his business to intercept the mail, picking out an airmail letter an easy task amongst so little correspondence anyway.

I waited until he'd closed the door behind him before opening the envelope. As one would expect the letter was typed on the solicitors' headed paper and formally written. It was dated a week ago.

> *"Dear Ms Theakston*
> ### *THE ESTATE OF JOHN ROBERT THEAKSTON*
> *We are acting on behalf of the estate of the above-named and understand you have been advised by the Endover Police Force, namely by a DCI Munroe of the tragic circumstances of*

the deaths of both your mother, Brenda Anne Theakston and of the above-named.

Please accept our condolences.

Under the terms of her Will, at the time of your mother's death her estate passed in its entirety to Mr Theakston with the proviso that should he predecease her, her estate would pass to the Sydney Animal Rescue Centre.

As, in law, a person may not benefit from their crime your mother's estate bypasses Mr Theakston and settles on the residuary beneficiary, that is, the animal charity."

What a bitch! I might have guessed that's what she'd do; she must really have hated me.

"Although Mr Theakston had made a small provision for you in his Will we have to advise that his estate was in considerable debt and we believe that once all his assets have been liquidised and his debts settled only a nominal amount will be left.

We will, of course, keep you advised of progress but in the meantime, we require various documentation and details from you as itemised on the accompanying sheet. We would

appreciate your swift response and will keep you
updated of progress.
Yours xxxxxx"

I read the letter over twice, once out loud to Liliad. 'Well, thanks a lot Mother and Father. Bastards to the end!' I still had a fair amount behind me, enough to support me whilst I carved out a new life for myself outside St Joseph's because 'outside' is where I intended to be and I wasn't going to wait much longer.

Sitting with Liliad on my lap I looked hard into her eyes. 'We need to think this through carefully, Liliad; we really do.'

◆

'Where do you think your parents will be buried?'

Alberto's question caught me by surprise, coming as it did during one of our illicit written English lessons.

'Why? Are you hoping for a trip to Australia?'

Alberto grinned completely transforming his features, his teeth a dazzling white against the blackness of his skin, even and of regular size; he'd be perfect for a toothpaste advertisement. 'In your dreams, Annalee; in your dreams.'

I couldn't believe the thought hadn't occurred to me before as what happened to my parents remains was of little interest but maybe that was a mistake; how they were disposed of could prove useful. I brought our lesson to an abrupt close and once Alberto had gone began to plan.

I arranged a meeting with Dr Chang.

'Thank you for seeing me at such short notice, Dr Chang.'

Dr Chang nodded, sat back in his chair with an air of patient authority, placed his hands up towards his face, finger tips together and waited for me to continue.

'I expect you're aware of my sad news.'

He nodded and gave a conciliatory smile. 'Yes, Annalee I am. I was very sorry; it must be a lot for you to deal with.'

'Yes, it has been but I think I'm slowly coming to terms with it.'

He said nothing, just waited. I hesitated as if feeling embarrassed and awkward at what I was about to say. 'Mm, it seems that I will benefit quite substantially from my father's Will.'

Dr Chang didn't respond except for an almost inaudible intake of breath indicative of a barely suppressed anticipation of something good to come. I wouldn't disappoint him.

'The thing is I've realised in recent weeks how lucky I've been to be here at St Joseph's. I mean the care and treatment I've received – more than I deserve I think in view of what I did to Dr Metcalfe.' I lowered my eyes and allowed a slight break in my voice. 'I'm truly sorry for that; I still don't really understand what happened, why I did it.'

Dr Chang gave a knowing smile. 'Accepting what you did was wrong is a huge step forward, content yourself with that for now.'

I gave Dr Chang a tearful nod of gratitude. 'Anyway as I said I'm going to come into some money once the solicitors have settled my father's estate and I'd like to make a gift to St Joseph's.' I hesitated as if a new thought had only just occurred to me. 'Or maybe a particular line of research, whatever you think best.'

Dr Chang squirmed slightly on his chair, excitement at the prospect of extra funding overriding any fear that he'd be accused of taking advantage of a vulnerable pa-tient. 'Well, that would be very generous, Annalee. I'm sure if I have a word with the trustees we can agree on a suitable use for any bequest. Mm, about how much were you thinking?'

I knew it, it was so easy, I could almost see the pound signs in his eyes. 'Oh, I can't really say until I know ex-actly what my inheritance is but it'll be a worthwhile sum, I'm sure.'

Dr Chang's smile was benevolence itself.

'I wonder if you could help me with something else, Dr Chang.'

'If I can.'

I laid my hands in my lap like a contrite, obedient schoolgirl. 'It's my parents' funerals. I've been in touch with the Australian solicitors and they tell me that neither of them made any stipulations in their Wills for how they wanted their remains dealt with. I realise, of course, that I wouldn't be allowed to travel to Australia to attend but I wondered, if I had their bodies brought back, do you think I'd be allowed to attend their funeral here? I'd expect to be supervised, have Alberto with me of course.'

I looked Dr Chang directly in the eyes, mine wide and pleading. 'I really need closure, Dr Chang; I need to be at their funeral otherwise it all seems so unreal.' Large tears formed in my eyes that I allowed to run down my cheeks unheeded. 'Please, Dr Chang, will you make the trustees understand?'

He hesitated only briefly. 'It seems a perfectly reasonable request in the circumstances and I see no valid reason why St Joseph's cannot accommodate it, you are greatly improved and your risk category is now considered low. I'll put it before the Board next week and let you know their decision although I don't anticipate any objections.'

Sniffling loudly I wiped my hand over my cheek dispelling the salt tears. 'Thank you, Dr Chang; thank you so much.'

A couple more months have passed and I'm well on the way to being redeemed in the eyes of the establishment. I'm still viewed with a degree of caution as it's generally believed that I did kill Dr Metcalfe's fiancée, Melissa which, strangely, seems harder for people to forgive than the killing of Dr Metcalfe himself.

However, my parents' violent deaths have mellowed a few hearts and heads and, coupled with Alberto's favourable reports on my behaviour have resulted in a lessening of the restrictions on me.

My request to have my parents bodies repatriated and be allowed to attend their funeral was unanimously approved by the Board of Trustees coming as it did with my promise of a sizeable bequest. I didn't rush putting the wheels in motion to get my parents bodies back to England claiming I needed time to organise finances to afford a decent funeral and pay all associated bills but now all is set for my next move.

Alberto, I knew, was massively in debt, his credit rating was abysmal; he wanted to go back to his family in Venezuela as his father was ill but on his salary and with his current financial mess it was the impossible dream. This was my lever.

'Alberto, how close are you to getting to Venezuela?'

He looked up from struggling with the English exercise I'd set him, his eyes dulled with sadness. 'Years I would think.'

'That long? Are your debts really that extensive?'

Alberto simply shrugged.

I chewed at my bottom lip, considering. If I judged Alberto wrongly it could make things difficult for me in future. I would need to feel my way slowly. 'You know, you've been very kind to me, it's made a huge difference to my time in St Joseph's; made it more bearable.'

Alberto shrugged. 'I'm just doing my job.'

'Yes, of course you are but it still matters.' I paused looking hard at Alberto, trying to gauge the extent of his integrity.

'How did you get into *so* much debt?'

He raised his head at an angle and looked at me out of hooded eyes. 'Why the interest?'

It was my turn to shrug. 'Just curious.'

He hesitated and then obviously deciding it wouldn't hurt said, 'Drugs.'

'Oh dear, you have been a naughty boy.' I grinned and was rewarded with a lop-sided grin in return.

'I was an idiot but I'm off them now.'

'But now you have your debts to repay; what are they for, rent, utilities, people you borrowed from?'

Alberto sighed, 'All of the above and some.'

I paused and turned to look out of the window, considering. 'I could help you,' I said quietly. Getting no response I turned to face him. Once again he was looking down at his exercise book. 'Alberto, I said I can help you.'

He looked up, a slightly bemused expression on his face. 'Why would you do that?'

'Because I know what it's like to feel trapped.' We looked at one another in silence for a few moments. I could sense he was tempted, at least so far as wanting to know what I was proposing. 'I'm coming into some money from my father's estate and I'm prepared to buy your airline ticket to Venezuela.'

Alberto's eyes widened. 'Really and why would you do that?'

'Because I want to get out of my trap too and I need your help to do that.'

He snorted. 'You can't be serious; why the hell would I do that; my career would be over before it had hardly begun.'

'True but then you won't need a career out in Venezuela will you? At least not this one; just think about it; no debts, back with your family, there for your dad in his final days; sun, sea and sand. What's not to like?'

He was silent, temptation snipping away at his conscience. I needed to cement the idea. 'I want to tell you why I killed Dr Metcalfe.'

Alberto straightened in his chair, giving me his full attention. I wondered if he knew the old adage about curiosity killing the cat. 'Dr Metcalfe sexually abused me during our therapy sessions. It had to stop … so I stopped him.'

Alberto gave a low whistle but didn't jump to Dr Metcalfe's defence which was encouraging. 'So why didn't you report him at the time?'

'No-one would have believed me; after all, I'd been convicted of killing his fiancée … some might even consider I deserved it.'

'And did you – deserve it?'

I looked steadily into Alberto's eyes. 'No, I did not because I truly did *not* kill his fiancée.'

'And you expect me to believe *that* as well?'

I sat on the edge of my bed facing Alberto and took a deep breath. 'You've been present at my meetings with Inspector Munroe, you must have noticed his animosity toward me; his almost sadistic pleasure when he gave me the news about my parents' deaths.'

Alberto nodded. 'I did think he could have broken the news a little less harshly.'

'Inspector Munroe has his own agenda. His daughter died in tragic circumstances a couple of years ago. We were friends, Lily and I, very close but he never liked our friendship, was always trying to stop it and when Lily died he blamed me although I had absolutely nothing to do with it. He tried to charge me but couldn't make anything stick; he had no proof because there was none. When Dr Metcalfe's fiancée died and he discovered I'd known her as well he fabricated evidence, put together a strong circumstantial case against me and, with Dr Metcalfe's help, got me put in here but I'm innocent, Alberto; I *swear* I'm innocent.'

I studied him intently. I could tell he harboured doubts at what I'd said but was balancing that against the prospect of shedding all his liabilities and heading for the sun. I just needed one more push. 'Alberto, I am *not* insane. I'm not a threat to anyone. I did *not* kill Dr Metcalfe's fiancée but I will never be able to prove that shut up in here. All I want is a chance to clear my name, to start a new life – as do you. I can get you to Venezuela where your debts can't follow you and you can be there for your dad. All I ask is that you help me right a terrible wrong. That's not so bad is it?'

Alberto's face was a picture of conflicting desires as he battled with his conscience. 'But you did kill Dr Metcalfe; how can I believe that you won't pose a threat outside St Joseph's?'

'Alberto, for God's sake what was I supposed to do? He was sexually abusing me, it'd gone on for almost a year. He was so powerful – Dr Metcalfe, the eminent psy-chiatrist, well-respected by all and you think the trustees would believe *me*; someone Dr Metcalfe had diagnosed as a psychopath! Get real, Alberto!'

Still looking down Alberto slowly nodded. 'So, what do you propose?'

I allowed myself a slight smile; the name Alberto means "beautiful by noble behaviour" – how wrong can some parents be!

CHAPTER 4

It had taken the Australian lawyers several months to settle my father's estate and I'd managed to have my parents bodies kept in cold storage all that time maintaining that, my situation being what it was, I had neither the money nor the necessary presence of mind to deal with their funerals any sooner.

The delay had given me ample time to plan my disappearance; getting Alberto on board was the final piece in the jigsaw and he'd proven a real asset. 'How did you get on with Dr Chang?'

He grinned back at me the flash of his white teeth in his dark face illuminating his features. 'Fine, just as you predicted. I asked him if he thought it'd be beneficial to let you have a few short trips outside before the funeral day – with me in attendance of course.'

'Of course, Alberto; I wouldn't dream of going anywhere without you!'

'I said I thought it'd make it easier for you, reduce the emotional stress if you didn't have to cope with the strangeness of being outside St Joseph's after so long plus the strain of the funeral.'

'And he agreed; just like that?'

'Not until I reminded him of your offered donation and that if you suffered a relapse due to the stress of it all he'd probably have to wait for his money.'

Now it was my turn to grin. 'You learn fast, Alberto. Well done.'

We used the trips Alberto had so cleverly negotiated to begin constructing my new identity. Using an internet café we searched the records for a female baby who had died on the day I was born and then sent in a request for the birth certificate. This was surprisingly easy presumably because people often mislay such items so no questions were asked.

I intended, when my money ran out, to work cash in hand at casual jobs and I felt the birth certificate would be a proof of identity that most people would accept if needed.

I'd rented a mail box facility and had all correspondence and Alberto's airline ticket to Venezuela delivered there. Over the months I'd slowly removed monies from my bank account in cash and placed it in a safe deposit box I'd rented in another bank so that when I absconded I could exist without leaving a money trail as the general public were mostly willing to accept cash that they could hide from the taxman.

Sitting in Alberto's car I went through the plan one last time. 'After the funeral ceremony you'll drive me to the mail box shop and I'll collect your airline ticket. You'll then drive me to the train station where I will hand the ticket over to you. We will then both go our separate ways and you will *never* try to contact or find me ever again. Do you understand, Alberto?'

Alberto nodded and our pact was sealed.

◆

The day of the funeral was cold, grey and raining causing people to bow their heads to the watery onslaught, taking little notice of what was going on around them – perfect. Only Alberto, I and the funeral directors were attending; I'd made it plain that I didn't want the 'support' of any St Joseph's staff and none of my parents' English friends had been in touch about funeral dates. I expect, learning of my father's crime and knowing that I was incarcerated in a psychiatric hospital they didn't feel inclined to be associated with such a family.

On one of our trips out I'd purchased a plain, black dress, matching coat, shoes, handbag etc. It felt strange as I put them on, it was as though I were already slipping into yet another persona and I had to concentrate to keep Annalee Theakston with me for just a little longer.

Alberto too had dressed for the occasion; in a sombre, grey suit he was more handsome than ever and I felt a slight twinge of regret that he would no longer be a part of my life.

Sitting in the back of the chauffeur driven funeral car with Alberto, Liliad on my lap the whole thing felt a little macabre; like we were the bride and groom at a Goth wedding. I noticed the driver kept glancing in his rear view mirror, perhaps slightly apprehensive at having a 'psycho' as his passenger. I had to stuff a hankie in my mouth to suppress the giggle that threatened to spill out of me.

Against tradition I insisted on Alberto and myself being seated in the front pew as the coffins arrived; I had no intention of dutifully following my parents up the aisle. Crematoriums don't seem to cater for two at once so one coffin was laid on the conveyor belt and the other on trestles beside it. I wondered who was going into the flames first and hoped it was my mother.

The celebrant I'd hired, a smart woman in her late thirties, shuffled uncomfortably at the lectern. Obviously more used to a bigger audience she kept giving anxious glances in my direction. We'd never actually met, I'd merely written her a few, a very few, words giving next to no details about my parents' lives from which the poor woman had tried to cobble together some form of eulogy but when she began speaking of family bonds I interrupted her. 'Perhaps we can just go on to the committal, please.'

Her relief was palpable and the whole thing was over in less than fifteen minutes.

As Alberto and I left the chapel our driver moved toward us. I lowered my head and dabbed at my eyes, hugging Liliad close to my breast. Quietly I begged that he allow me a few moments to wander the Gardens of Remembrance before we headed back. The weather being like it was he was only too happy to take up Alberto's suggestion of a few moments inside with a cup of coffee. As I started toward the formal gardens I noticed his look of incredulity that a grown woman needed to cuddle a doll for comfort and he turned his back on me with relief.

Alberto soon caught up with me. 'My car's over by the back gates as we agreed,' he said as he fell in alongside me. We both quickened our pace until we were almost jogging the last few yards. Fumbling in his pocket for the key Alberto pressed the remote and the car flashed into life.

Gratefully I sank onto the front passenger seat, settling Liliad on my lap. My feet were throbbing; running in heeled dress shoes was not a good idea. Alberto dropped into the seat beside me bringing the smell of cold and damp in with him. The rain of earlier had increased so that drops clung to his suit and glistened on his wiry, black hair. He turned the key and as the engine grumbled he turned on the heater and taking a brief glance in the rear view and wing mirrors he pulled smoothly away from the kerb and headed toward town.

By the time we arrived at the Mail Box shop it was getting close to lunchtime. Alberto kept the engine running as I entered the shop and reclaimed the items I'd stored. As soon as I returned, he pulled away heading for the train station. He kept glancing down at the objects on my lap, a nervousness making his driving slightly erratic. I laid a hand gently on his arm, 'It's OK, Alberto; it's all here as I promised – your new life is about to start.' I smiled reassuringly and was rewarded with a brief nod of his head in confirmation.

Pulling into the train station car park he turned off the engine and swivelled in his seat to look at me intently. 'Where will you go?'

'Oh, I'm not going to tell you that. Here,' I handed him the two packages; one a thin envelope containing his plane ticket, the other an A4 padded envelope containing some cash. 'To tide you over,' I said in answer to his silent question.

He took them from my hand. 'Aren't you going to open them?'

He shook his head. 'No need.'

'OK,' I smiled, 'thanks for that vote of confidence, Alberto; in fact, thanks for everything. Have a good life out in Venezuela.' I picked my handbag up from the foot-well and, cuddling Liliad, made to get out of the car. Alberto laid a hand on my shoulder.

'Take care, Annalee.'

I calculated there was a very slight risk that Alberto would take the ticket and money as evidence of my duplicitous behaviour and then report me to the authorities to gain a bundle of brownie points for his career. He could claim I'd given him the slip and absconded after the funeral but I didn't think he would. As our plans had progressed he'd become more enthusiastic at the prospect of such a marked change in his circumstances. On balance I reckoned I was safe but nonetheless I wasn't going to leave anything to chance.

I nodded and left without a backward glance. Hurrying into the railway station I stopped just inside the entrance and waited until I saw Alberto drive away before heading to the bank where I collected the cash I'd been depositing. Stuffing five hundred pounds into my handbag I placed the rest inside a plastic bag and then inside the foldaway carrier bag I'd hidden in the inside pocket of my coat and carefully placing Liliad on top of it all I retraced my steps to the station, obtained a one-way ticket from the machine and caught the one thirty train to London.

CHAPTER 5

Keeping my head down, I walked as quickly as I could out of Kings Cross station. I knew from past experience that the police would access the station's security cameras and may well pick me out however hard I tried to be inconspicuous. Once outside I turned left toward a small boutique that I knew specialised in clothes that were quite different to the tailored, classic outfit of my funeral attire.

Half an hour later, staring at my reflection in the fitting room mirror I assessed my new look. Mid-calf length full, brightly patterned skirt, short suede jacket, polo neck white silken sweater and a large brimmed floppy brown hat that when worn at a rakish angle covered most of my face. The only thing needed to complete the outfit was knee high fashion boots and I knew just the shop for those. Paying in cash I watched as the shop assistant neatly folded the garments and placed them in a carrier bag. 'Thanks so much for your help; I'm sure my niece will be thrilled.'

'It's lucky you're almost identical in size; being able to try on a whole outfit it's so much easier to see if it really goes.'

'My thoughts exactly; I only wish we lived closer, I'd love to borrow some of her clothes.' I grinned as I hefted the bag towards me. As I did so the carrier bag containing my bulk cash and Liliad slipped out of my grasp onto the counter. The assistant moved to grab it as it keeled over just as one of Liliad's arms flopped out the top. I instinctively snatched at the handle, practically slapping the assistant's hand out of the way. 'Leave it!'

The assistant took a step back surprised at my tone. 'I'm sorry, I was only trying to help.'

I tucked Liliad's arm back inside and drew the bag into my arms. 'No, I'm sorry, I didn't mean to snap. It's just the doll is extremely delicate and can so easily be damaged.' I smiled in apology.

'No problem; I understand.' Looking enviously at me as I walked toward the exit, picking up on our previous conversation, she commented, 'I'd have to starve for a week to have any chance of getting into my daughter's things,' and sighing resignedly she plonked onto the stool behind the counter as I let the door swing shut behind me.

I retraced my steps to the main road and hailed a taxi for Oxford Street. Entering one of the large department stores I found the ladies room and changed into my new outfit. I then made my way to the store's shoe department and spent a pleasurable half an hour trying on various boot styles until I was satisfied.

I knew that out the back of the store were a collection of recycle bins. I left by the back exit and threw the whole bag of my funeral clothes into the relevant bin – may some Third World woman have the benefit – it was nothing to me. I then took another taxi to Waterloo Station and bought a one-way ticket to Bournemouth.

◆

Once on the train I settled back into my seat, closed my eyes and allowed myself a few deep, calming breaths. As the train pulled away I gazed unseeing out of the window as my thoughts turned inwards towards the future and the new persona I was to adopt.

My new name was Coral Wright; I was really pleased by that, it had a lovely ring to it and I felt the clothes I'd chosen fitted the name well. I imagined her as a free spirit; a delicate butterfly fluttering through life; never alighting long enough to be trapped and pinned down. Absent-mindedly I picked up the hem of my flouncy skirt with my fingertips and, like a little girl, swirled it gently under cover of the train table. Silly I know but a pleasing sensation of freedom after the restriction of the funeral clothes and the dowdy uniform I was obliged to wear in St Joseph's. As the train passed through a tunnel I smiled at my reflection in the darkened window and mouthed silently, 'Hello Coral, nice to meet you.'

Pressing myself into the gentle curve of the back of the seat I lay my head against the headrest, closed my eyes once more and allowed my mind to drift back over the years.

I recalled the isolation of my childhood; my mother's cold, appraising stare each time she looked at me; the lack of any physical affection from her. Well, that was explained now, wasn't it. No wonder she hated the very sight of me – living evidence of her betrayal of her marriage. What must it have been like, living that lie for over thirty years; keeping up the pretence of a happy family? As the image of that cold, impregnable face floated into my mind I felt myself physically recoil, even though she was now no more than a pile of ash scattered to the winds.

Then there was my father, cuckolded and duped; no wonder he'd flipped when he'd finally found out. Looking back I had to admit he'd never been actively unkind to me, just indifferent but he was mostly like that toward my elder brother, Matt too. I guess he just wasn't cut out for family life and kids.

I sighed as the image of Matt's handsome face came to the fore. The only one who'd ever shown me affection my brother, fifteen years my senior, had been the mainstay of my life but then he'd met Addie and was planning to leave me. I was nine years old and distraught at the prospect. How could he abandon me and for *her*; so unlike me in every respect that I'd felt rejected twice over. I'd had to use all my cunning to rid myself of her; persuading her to take a swim in what I knew was a dangerous part of the river was a stroke of genius. I folded my arms across my middle and hugged into myself acknowledging my childhood cleverness but it all went wrong when Inspector Munroe came on the scene.

I could still picture him so vividly as he was when he first set foot in our house, the image so precise that I swear I could scent the smell of his pipe tobacco as though he were sitting beside me. I'm convinced that his relentless pursuit of Matt and his ardent conviction that Matt was guilty of harming Addie was what drove Matt to take his own life. It was thanks to Munroe that I no longer had my brother and for that he'd had to pay.

A loud thud of a duffle bag being slung onto the table in front jolted me out of my reverie. Startled, my eyes sprang open as a man in his early twenties, his hair cut short like an American GI and a gold stud near the edge of one eyebrow, dropped onto the seat opposite. He grinned, 'Did I wake you?'

I stared disapprovingly back. 'You could have been a little more considerate.'

He shrugged. 'And you could have booked into the Quiet Carriage near the front if it matters so much.' He rummaged in his bag, produced a mobile and set of earphones and plugged himself in ignoring the angry look I gave. He lolled back in his seat at an angle, stretching his long legs out toward the aisle and leaving his duffle bag on the table between us like a barrier.

Considering him with cold detachment I moved my right leg under the table to rest more securely against the carrier bag that contained my money and Liliad. I'm sure she was none too pleased to be so confined for the entire journey but I didn't dare bring her out to sit on my lap; it would have drawn unwanted attention and in any case would be picked up on the train's CCTV. I knew I'd have a lot of making up to do once we reached Bournemouth.

◆

Pulling into the station I deliberately waited until the young man opposite had left. Bending down to pull my carrier bag out from under the table I caught sight of a black wallet that had slid under the opposite seat. Ducking under the table I was just able to reach it, dragging it toward me with my fingertips. It must belong to the young man; I recalled how he'd slung his jacket onto the seat as he sat down. It must have fallen out of his pocket. I glanced out of the window as I tucked the wallet into my handbag spotting him hurrying back along the platform, his hands delving in his pockets as he did so, his face a picture of confusion and mounting anxiety. I grinned, muttering under my breath, 'Serve you right, you obnoxious little prick.'

I gathered my bags about me and made my way out. As I went to step onto the platform the young man leaped up into the carriage beside me. 'Have you seen a wallet near where I was sitting?' his voice raising an octave in panic.

'Why, have you lost one?'

'Well obviously.' he snapped.

'No, I haven't.' I smiled as I stepped down from the train. It didn't bother me to know the difficulties I was causing him and not just because he'd been so unpleasant. I wouldn't have cared even if he'd been the nicest person on the planet. As I saw it, the wallet was there for the taking; I might as well have it as anyone else.

I made my way to the exit. As the machine swallowed my ticket and the barrier opened I stepped through into my new life. Taxis waited in line like a row of black beetles; I was pleased to see so many Hackney cabs; I always feel so much more dignified sitting in their spacious interiors. 'Just to the seafront, please; anywhere along there will do.'

The driver nodded and coasted out of the station fore-court whilst I settled back to consider my next step. It was still early in the year, the holiday season hadn't really begun so I didn't anticipate any problem getting a room in a B & B and there were copious numbers of those along the front. It would do for a couple of weeks whilst I searched for an apartment to rent.

I'd chosen Bournemouth as I considered it a good place in which to disappear. Sprawling and large it had a transient population due to being a holiday destination mixed with its long-term residents and there was plenty of part-time casual work available especially during the holiday period so I shouldn't have too much difficulty supplementing my finances. It was also twenty five to thir-ty miles from Dorchester where my mother had worked and, it seems, had her illicit affair. I figured the authorities would be trying to find me, at least for a while and with Inspector Munroe's knowledge of those intimate details of my family life they might well direct at least part of their search in that area. I would have to be very careful when making my own enquiries.

'This do you, luv?' The taxi driver pulled over to the kerb.

'Yes, that's fine, how much?'

'£5 to you.'

I handed over the cash.

'Have a nice stay.'

I picked up my bags and stepped out of the cab. He'd dropped me at the start of the seafront walk. I took a few deep breaths, luxuriating in the fresh air and tang of saltiness and started to walk slowly along, assessing the B & B's as I went.

I didn't want one that looked too upmarket, partly due to price but also I was concerned they may be more particular about recording personal details but neither did I want anything that risked lowered cleanliness standards. Eventually I settled on one called The Roselea Hotel.

A woman in her forties opened the door to my ring. About five foot six, a little overweight and bearing a duster in her right hand she had an air of motherliness that bode well. I smiled my most deprecating smile and politely asked, 'I wonder if I might rent a room for a couple of weeks please.' As I spoke I directed my eyes to the 'Vacancies' notice in the front window, an unspoken challenge to a refusal.

She eyed me up and down taking in my attire, my handbag and my one large carrier bag obviously questioning in her mind how anyone with so little luggage could be requesting a room for two weeks. I regrouped quickly. 'The rest of my things are at the station property office. I thought I'd find somewhere first and then collect them; I didn't want to be dragging it all around with me.'

This explanation seemed to satisfy her as she stood back from the door, inviting me in. I followed her down the long hallway to a reception desk of dark, burnished wood that smelt as though it had recently been polished; the scent tickling my nose, threatening a sneeze.

'I've a single room out the back; it's not very big but it's cosy and warm, which in this weather you might appreciate. It's reasonably priced at £70 per night, including breakfast. There's a residents lounge on the ground floor and breakfast is served seven to nine-thirty.'

'That sounds fine; thank you.'

She took a key off the rack behind her then turned back to the desk swivelling a Guest Book round to face me. 'Just write name and address details and I'll require the two weeks paid in advance.'

I obediently signed Coral Wright and wrote a fictitious address, then counted out the cash. She took the money and tucked it into her apron pocket. 'If you'd care to follow me; you'll find it's very quiet here; we're a little way off our really busy time. What brings you to Bournemouth ahead of the holiday season?'

'Oh, just the need for a little time to myself combined with sea air therapy.'

'Well, you'll certainly get both here. The wind can blow off the sea pretty hard when it has a mind to.'

We reached the first floor landing and continued along its length to a door at the very end, passing two other doors on the way. The carpet, as on the stairs, was highly patterned in a 1940's deep red, floral design obviously of high quality with a good underlay; our feet barely made a whisper as we passed along. As she unlocked the door the sun emerged from behind clouds illuminating the room as though she'd just switched on a light. Instantly I could feel the warmth of the sun's rays intensified as they passed through the window glass.

'As I said a small but very cosy room,' she stood to one side to let me pass. 'I'll leave you to sort yourself out. You're welcome to use the residents lounge whenever you want. The front door is locked at night by eleven so if you intend coming back after then you'll need to ring the bell. I've a gentleman who does the night shift so he'll let you in.' She handed me my room key. 'My name's Dorothy by the way but everyone calls me Dot.' She took a final glance around the room as though assuring herself all was in order then left, quietly closing the door behind her.

I dropped my handbag and carrier onto the bed and flopped down beside them, gently extricating Liliad from her confinement. Carefully untangling her strings I sat her on the bed beside me and smoothed my hand over her ruffled hair. 'Well, Liliad so far so good. I think this will do well until we can get a place of our own.'

As I turned Liliad's head toward me the sunshine caught her eyes, intensifying the blackness of her pupils that seemed to spread like ink on paper until they appeared unnaturally large; drawing me in to their comforting warm depths, giving me the reassurance I needed that I was following the right path.

I bounced up and down on the bed a little, pleased at the springiness of the mattress which bode well for a good night's sleep. The bed was positioned close to the window with a bedside cabinet on the window side creating just enough space to walk around it. To my right as I sat on the bed was another door standing open which revealed an en suite shower room and to my left was a free standing wardrobe and chest of drawers on which stood a television and coffee/tea making facilities. One easy chair was positioned at the foot of the bed and a sheepskin rug lay by the bed in addition to the carpet. All looked and smelt delightfully clean.

I opened the carrier bag and extracted four hundred pounds which I put into my handbag. Placing Liliad on my lap I tilted her head so that I held her gaze. 'I'm going to have to put you in the wardrobe while I'm out; I can't risk you being discovered because if there's anything in the media about my disappearance they're likely to mention you too and we can't risk any connection but I'll see about getting us somewhere of our own as soon as I can and then it'll be like old times, when we were in our flat in Endover. You do understand, don't you?'

Liliad's head dropped forward slightly in acknowledgement; I could tell she was unhappy but accepted the need for such caution. 'OK, I'm going to put you in the wardrobe now and pop out to buy myself some more clothes and open a safe deposit box again so I can keep the money somewhere safe. I promise I'll be as quick as I can.' I hugged her close, hating having to shut her away again especially after all she'd been through at St Joseph's but there was no choice. As I quietly shut the wardrobe door I whispered, 'I'll make it right; I promise.'

CHAPTER 6

Bournemouth shopping centre, even on this cold unchar-
itable day, seemed to thrum with people, so many more
than the relative quiet of Endover. I pulled my jacket closer
about me as I silently determined that my first purchase
would be a warm coat, scarf and gloves. I also needed to
buy a suitcase to put it all in so that I could arrive back at
the B & B looking as though I'd just retrieved it from the
railway station property office.

Once I'd deposited my cash into a safe deposit box
facility at the bank I headed for the shops, spending all
of the four hundred pounds I'd set aside. It was annoying having to spend so much when I had perfectly good
clothes in storage back in Endover, there being no need

for a fashion wardrobe in St Joseph's, but I considered it a fair price for my freedom.

Making the suitcase my final item I piled all my carrier bags into it and, suddenly realising how hungry I was, found a charming little Italian restaurant.

I chose a table deep inside so I could sit with my back against the wall and peruse the whole area, my suitcase tucked out of the way by my side. I ordered a lasagne and salad with a large glass of Chablis to wash it down. As I sipped my wine and waited for my meal to be served I contemplated the other diners. There was quite a mix; a family of four tucking into their meals with enthusiasm despite all being grossly overweight, obviously not something that concerned them. There were three tables that looked like the proverbial 'ladies that lunch' set and a couple of men in suits dining out on expenses. There may have been a few holidaymakers but it was hard to tell when everyone was so wrapped up against the cold. Over by the window were a couple of tables occupied by some of Bournemouth's many retirees. All in all, quite an eclectic mix and one in which I should be able to disappear with ease.

My meal arrived and I ordered another large glass of wine reasoning that this was something of a celebration albeit a solitary one. Concentrating on eating I didn't notice the new arrival until, almost finished, I paused to glance around the restaurant once more. The shock I felt at sight of the person just taking his seat at a table four rows down from me was so intense I thought for a dreadful moment that I might faint. I screwed my eyes tight shut, opened them again, praying that I was mistaken; that he was simply a lookalike. It was no good; I'd never forget that handsome face. The five or six years since I'd last seen him had done him no disservice; if anything he had improved with maturity. Still tall and powerfully built his strong jawline was now defined by a close cut beard that emphasised chiselled features. The subdued lighting in the restaurant made it impossible for me to see his eyes but if they'd retained their thick lashes and dark depths I could imagine the whole package was mesmerising. 'My God, Barry Mason'.

I shuffled further back in my seat, trusting to the ambient lighting to shield me, and let my mind drift back over the years. Barry had been one of my students during my time at Endover College. He was nineteen then, with an assured cockiness and belief in his sexual magnetism – not exactly misplaced in my opinion. I'd played him like a puppet; manipulating him into a relationship with Inspector Munroe's daughter, Lily. It hadn't lasted; I'd managed to generate too much bad feeling on all sides for that but it had served its purpose in that it had got under Munroe's skin like poison ivy. Weaving a web that had trapped

Barry and Lily it enabled me to punish Munroe for his part in my brother's death. It was a game I'd enjoyed and I knew its sticky threads still clung to Munroe, Lily's death ensured that.

None of my musing however solved my current dilemma – what the hell was Barry Mason doing in Bournemouth? The last I'd heard was that he'd returned to his roots in Sheffield to work at an animal sanctuary. The problem was I didn't know how much, if anything, Barry knew of my involvement in his past problems and Lily's death. Despite the unlikelihood of his having maintained any connection with the Munroe family I couldn't risk him discovering me.

As silently as I could I rose and made my way to the ladies cloakroom. Once there I donned my outdoor clothes and replaced my hat being careful to position it low so that the brim covered part of my face. As I left the ladies I look around for another exit but having no choice other than to walk through the restaurant to get out I hastened to take a route as far away from Barry's table as possible.

I was just approaching the row at which he was sitting when my wheeled suitcase caught on an empty chair sending it crashing to the ground in a crescendo of metallic clatter. It seemed that everyone in the restaurant gasped in surprise and before I could make my escape Barry had risen from his seat and was picking up and replacing the offending chair. I gave a muffled 'Thank you' and keeping my face averted scurried out the door almost managing, in my haste, to hook the suitcase around that as well. With Barry's eyes following my steps I dodged the traffic and hurried toward the seafront and the sanctuary of my B & B.

◆

'I see you've collected your luggage.' The landlady sat behind her desk, a newspaper spread out in front of her. 'I hope it isn't too heavy, it's a decent walk from the station.'

I gave her a slightly quizzical look.

'I didn't see a taxi pull up,' she explained.

'Oh, right. No, it isn't too heavy.' I headed toward the stairs as she returned to her newspaper.

'It's terrible that M25 isn't it?'

'I beg your pardon.'

She pointed at a photograph on an inside page. 'Just terrible; another young life ruined I expect and there was him probably looking forward to his holiday.'

'Why do you say that?'

'Well, it stands to reason doesn't it; he was heading towards Heathrow apparently.' She sighed and closed the paper, getting up from the desk. 'Better start thinking about getting myself some tea.'

I hesitated for a second debating with myself whether I was just being silly and then decided that I wouldn't rest until I knew. 'Mm, have you finished with the paper?'

'Yes, why, would you like it?'

'If you don't mind; I enjoy doing the crosswords,' I said by way of explanation.

'Be my guest.' She folded it in half and handed it to me.

I tucked it under my arm and continued up the stairs. Once in my room I propped the suitcase against the wall and immediately extracted Liliad from the wardrobe. Sitting her beside me on the bed I opened the paper, scanning the pages for the article the landlady had been reading.

'Oh, my God!' I found the item on page four. It barely took up two column inches but the photograph was enough. Alberto's car, I was sure it was his as I could clearly see the image of the Venezuelan flag he'd had painted on the driver door, lay on its roof; a badly crumpled van alongside it.

It was clear from the text that the landlady had merely looked at the photograph of battered vehicles and not read the article which stated that the driver had been identified from his driving licence and was the young man involved in the recent disappearance of a patient from the St Joseph's Psychiatric Hospital in Endover. From an airline ticket found in his belongings it appeared that he was planning to flee the country.

I turned to Liliad. 'It says here that he's in a critical condition; a fifty-fifty chance of pulling through. Damn! Why couldn't he have just died?'

Liliad's eyelids drooped so that she was observing me through narrowed slits, her nose wrinkling slightly giving her the appearance of an Oriental cat.

'Why couldn't he have just got on that plane; it was *all* he had to do.' I couldn't keep the exasperation out of my tone. 'After all, we don't want him getting well enough to *talk*, do we?'

Liliad shrugged her shoulders, making me consider further.

'Well, I suppose there isn't much he can say that would be damaging. They've probably already worked out what happened, the sequence of events and he'd no idea where we were headed; I'd made sure of that. Hopefully they've picked me up on King's Cross Station CCTV and believe I'm still in London.'

I'd decided that my priority was to find Liliad and I a flat of our own to rent where I could close the door and relax and Liliad didn't have to spend hours stuck inside a wardrobe, an arrangement which was proving far from conducive to a harmonious relationship.

I wanted to remain as close to the sea front and town centre as I could so I'd always have the choice of walking or public transport. I didn't really want to go through an estate agent as the less scrutiny I had of my personal details the better so instead I scoured the local papers, eventually settling on a two bedroom furnished flat two roads back from the sea front. The current owner was offering it as a short-term holiday let which he managed himself but when I put down a hefty deposit in cash and agreed the rent with no haggling he was only too pleased to change his plans and allow a six month let with the option to extend, thus saving him the frequent change-over chores.

The flat was on the fourth floor of a purpose-built block looking out toward a sea that I could just glimpse between the house roofs opposite but it had the advantage of being south facing so caught the sun for most of the day making it bright and cheery. Knowing how much Liliad loved to look out, I immediately positioned an easy chair by the window and placed her in it, a cushion behind her back for comfort. 'There, that's better isn't it?' I was rewarded with a smile that stretched from ear to ear and I knew our relationship was on the right track once more.

The flat was well equipped as one would expect from a holiday let. 'I think we'll be very happy here, Liliad,' I said as I opened a bottle of Chenin Blanc that evening and raised a glass. 'To our future; may it be everything we desire. Oh, I forgot; I've bought you a gift; well it's for both of us really.' I picked up the bag I'd placed on the sideboard and with a flourish pulled out a chess board and pieces. 'I'm afraid it's not a particularly posh set but it's small enough to transport. Once we've settled for good I'll invest in one of quality.'

I placed the board on the window cill in front of us and laid out the pieces. Enclosing a black and a white pawn in each hand I held them out to Liliad. 'Choose. OK, you're white, you make the first move.' We played for about an hour before I begged tiredness.

Later enjoying a luxurious soak in the bath I closed my eyes and recalled the many games of chess I'd played with my brother, Matt. He'd taught me the basics but my natural aptitude for strategy and tactics soon turned me into a formidable opponent despite out fifteen year age gap. We'd had a beautiful set, the pieces made of the finest rosewood and mahogany. I loved the feel of the pieces in my hands; their smooth curvatures, crenelated and domed tops but my favourite piece was the queen; I regarded her as the real power piece on the board. I *never* relinquished my queen.

Waking to a sunny morning and the screech of seagulls I felt confident that the future would be as bright as the day. Sitting beside Liliad as we resumed our game of the previous evening I gazed at the street below, watching people pass by on their way to work and feeling grateful that I no longer had such an enormous restriction on my time. I'd enough money to last me quite a while and if everything went according to plan I was convinced that the daily grind would remain a thing of the past.

Just at that moment I noticed a black man crossing the street a few yards down from my viewpoint and, as if chiding me for my complacency, my mind immediately brought forward an image of Alberto. I looked at Liliad, her eyes were also focussed on the young black man. 'I wonder how he is.'

Liliad's head moved fractionally toward me, she knew immediately who I meant, her eyes reflecting my question back to me.

I had no idea of the hospital with an A & E department nearest to Heathrow, which was presumably where he'd been taken. I grabbed my smartphone and asked Google the question. 'Hillingdon,' I said out loud as I jotted down the telephone number and address. The next question was what to do with the information. Did I need to do anything? Was there really anything of value that Alberto could tell the authorities assuming he was well enough to tell them anything? I closed my eyes, trying to picture each stage of our conspiracy. He could tell them I'd bribed him with money and the airline ticket; that I'd organised mail box and safe deposit box facilities; that I'd slowly withdrawn money from my bank account to keep as cash; that he'd dropped me at Endover train station but with no idea of where I was heading. Maybe I was being paranoid; worrying unnecessarily but then it hit, like the shock of someone throwing a bucket of iced water over me, my false identity; the internet café where I'd accessed my new name to acquire the birth certificate of Coral Wright. Had he known the name I'd adopted? My brow furrowed as I stared at Liliad for the answer but that was pointless, how could she know? She hadn't been with us but had been forced to remain in St Joseph's. It was so frustrating, I just couldn't remember and I knew what I was like. That seed of doubt would root itself deep in my subconscious, an annoying tendril that needed cutting at its root.

Feeling angry with Alberto for putting me through this and after all I'd done for him too. I reached for my smartphone again and looked up the trains from Bournemouth to Waterloo and then the buses from Waterloo to Hillingdon Hospital.

Once I'd made the decision I felt better and decided to take a walk into town. Choosing a smart looking hair salon I made an appointment for the next morning to have my hair dyed blonde and to have extensions fitted. I wanted this change to be permanent; no more itchy wigs and frequent costume changes.

Although chilly the sun was shining encouraging me to take a detour through the gardens that led down to the seafront. Crocuses and daffodils were just shouldering their way through the cold soil, as though called forth by the false promise of warmth from a bright but frigid sun. I continued down toward the sea relishing the open air and wide vista after the months coped up inside the claustrophobic atmosphere of St Joseph's.

As the path began its descent I had the uncanny sensation that I was not alone. I could hear my own steps as my heels struck the tarmac but there seemed, a brief second later, a hushed echo. I stopped and turned just as a dense cloud moved slowly over the sun, its shadow oozing over the gardens toward me like a roiling slick of viscous mud. I shuddered as the gloom passed over but could see no-one on the path near me.

Even so I quickened my pace onto the wider expanse of the promenade and entered the first café I came to. Ordering a large black coffee I positioned myself near the middle of the room with a clear view out of the window.

As the minutes ticked by I assessed the situation; was someone following me? I wasn't concerned just a little curious at my reaction but decided it was probably just some strange acoustics.

I sat for another thirty minutes before making my way back to the flat. Liliad was where I'd left her, watching the world go by. I slumped into the chair opposite. 'I've just been really silly,' I began, 'I thought I was being followed but it was just my imagination.'

Liliad looked at me thoughtfully.

'But it's taught me one thing; I need to know the position with Alberto, to silence him if necessary; I don't like loose ends.'

Liliad simply stared.

◆

Deciding there was no time like the present, I telephoned Hillingdon Hospital the next morning. 'Hello, I'm enquiring after an Alberto Jackman. He was involved in a road traffic accident near Heathrow Airport recently. Is he in Hillingdon Hospital?'

'I'll put you through to Admissions.'

I heard a number of clicks and then, 'Admissions.'

I repeated my question.

'Yes, he's still in the Intensive Care Unit. Are you a relative?'

'No, I'm just a close friend.'

'Then I'm afraid I can't tell you any more than that.'

'I understand; thanks for your help.' I ended the call before I could get any awkward questions. 'Well, that settles it, Liliad, a trip to Hillingdon is called for but first I need to get my hair altered.'

◆

Three hours later, looking at my reflection in the salon mirror even I was taken aback by the dramatic change in my appearance the blonde dye and extensions made; I was a completely different person. As I stared I could feel Annalee Theakston slipping away as Coral Wright took her place.

The stylist stood behind me, admiring her handiwork as she too stared into the mirror. 'I must admit I wasn't too sure when you booked but you were right; it really suits you.'

I grinned back, nodding in agreement. As I left the salon it was as though a weight had been lifted off me and not just because I believed no-one from my past was likely to recognise me now. I'd managed to hide it from Inspector Munroe and had even partly convinced myself that it didn't matter but discovering I was not my father's daughter had actually come as a real shock and had unsettled me. Munroe had been correct in his sarcasm when he'd commented that I wasn't who I thought I was. It will be interesting to see how close to my biological father I really am but before I can begin that search I need to silence Alberto.

❖

Next morning I was up early ready to catch the train to Waterloo Station. I knew it was a frequent service and also that the buses to Hillingdon Hospital ran approximately every fifteen minutes from Waterloo. It would be a long day especially as I couldn't foretell how things would pan out.

Liliad was somewhat uncommunicative; I couldn't decide whether she'd just taken umbrage that she was to be left on her own all day or because she was concerned about what I was doing. 'It'll be fine; no-one will recognise me now,' I flounced my long tresses to illustrate the point, 'and I'll be very careful.'

Liliad's head turned slightly to look out of the window, effectively ignoring me. I sighed, 'So you think I should leave well alone?' Getting no response I gave up. 'Well, I don't.' So saying, I picked up my handbag, pulled on my fleece and left.

The journey passed smoothly and I arrived at the hospital just before lunch. Standing studying the board showing the floor layout of the hospital I located the Intensive Care Unit. Hurrying along the corridor concentrating on the various directional signs I became aware, just in front of me, of a couple of men in a huddle, deep in conversation. Going by his white coat one was obviously a doctor, the other, although he had his back to me I recognised instantly. It was Inspector Munroe, his shoulders slightly hunched over as he listened intently to what the much shorter doctor was saying. Stopped in my tracks I looked round frantically for an escape, desperate to get out of view before Munroe turned around.

I'd just passed a small kiosk staffed by volunteers selling magazines, newspapers and a selection of confectionary. I retraced my steps and entered, pretending to browse the various items, my eyes constantly darting up the corridor to where Munroe and the doctor still stood. Their discussion over they shook hands, the doctor going deeper into the hospital as Munroe headed toward the exit which would take him directly past the kiosk.

I plucked a bar of chocolate off the shelf and turned to the woman behind the counter to pay so that my back was to the corridor. The click clack of Munroe's shoes grew louder as he approached. I waited, my ears straining, praying for the sound to decrease as he passed and walked on. Suddenly there was silence, the tapping of his shoes stopped. A trickle of sweat ran down my back; he was standing directly behind me.

I ducked my head down so that my long hair hid my face and turned to the left, hoping to sidle past him.

'Don't forget your change, love.' The woman behind the counter held the fifty pence piece out toward me. My heart was thumping so loud in my head outside noise was muffled, as if my ears were stuffed with cotton wool. I snatched the coin from her fingers and fled as Munroe stepped toward the counter, a newspaper in his hand.

Hastening down the corridor I rounded a corner and sank onto the first available seat. Closing my eyes I took a few deep, controlled breaths as I tried to restore my equilibrium. Perhaps Liliad had been correct implying my visit was too risky; this had been much too close for comfort but I was here now and I wasn't going to go home empty-handed.

Steadied enough I continued on, locating the Intensive Care Unit easily. Peering through the glass at the top of the ward doors I could see two occupied beds, neither of which held Alberto. The bed nearest the door on the right was shrouded by curtains so I could only assume that was where he lay.

'Can I help you?'

I flinched and turned toward the nurse; she smiled enquiringly.

'Yes, I was looking for Alberto, Alberto Jackman.'

'Are you a relative?'

'No just a close friend; we worked together. How is he?'

'Not too good I'm afraid. It was a bad accident.'

I forced my lower lip to tremble as I asked, 'Have his parents been to see him?'

The nurse shook her head.

'I see; I expect they've not been able to get here, they live in Venezuela. It's *so sad*, no-one to even visit him.'

The nurse set her lips in a thin line, considering. 'Have you come far?'

'Yeah, it's been a long journey.' I sighed and shrugged my shoulders in resignation.

'You're right, it is sad that he hasn't had any visitors other than the police, poor lad – not that they could talk to him, they're still waiting for him to regain consciousness.' She hesitated for a moment longer, 'I can let you have just a few minutes.'

'Thank you.'

She pushed open the door and led me to Alberto's bed. Before pulling back the curtain she said, 'I should warn you, he's still unresponsive but we think he can hear us so try to talk to him, encourage him to make an effort, he needs to work with us if he's going to pull through this.'

I nodded and stepped up to the bed, the nurse pulling the curtain back into place as she left.

Alberto was wired up to several machines that beeped a continuous rhythmic presence such that one would be forgiven for believing that only technology was keeping him alive yet from what the nurse had said it seemed they believed Alberto only needed some real incentive to call him back from the abyss.

I pulled up a chair close to the bed and settling myself lent forward close enough that my breath caressed Alberto's cheek as I whispered in his ear. 'Hello, Alberto you've made a mess of things, haven't you? What a prize prat you are; all you had to do was get on that plane.' I paused, tweaking the cannula that was in the back of his hand and was rewarded by a slight twitch and a brief flutter of his eyelids. 'Oh, so you can feel something; the nurse says you can hear too. Well, let me tell you what's going to happen to you if you get well enough to leave here.

I know the police have just been and they're going to want to know all about our little escapade and they're not going to look too kindly on you, are they? After all, you've helped a dangerous psychopath escape back into the community; that has to be a big no, no.' I tweaked the cannula a little harder this time causing Alberto's hand to jerk slightly and a soft moan to escape from his lips.

'I can see a lengthy prison sentence looming and a pretty boy like you … I expect you'll be quite popular with the other inmates. And your parents, what on earth are they going to think after all the sacrifices they must have made to get you your airfare here in the first place; just think of the disgrace – will they ever be able to hold their heads up again? Do you really want to put them through all that? Wouldn't it be kinder to just let go; to fade away and leave them their dignity? The alternative doesn't bear thinking about, does it, Alberto?'

As I watched a tiny tear oozed from Alberto's eye; I took out a tissue and gently wiped it away from the stubble on his cheek. I paused again, giving him time to digest my words. 'And then there's me, Alberto; you have to understand my predicament; I mean, you were with me through all the planning, those visits to the internet café. You've got to realise that I can't take the risk of your saying anything that would help trace me.'

I could see Alberto's face tense slightly, a sure sign that he was hearing me. 'The thing is I really don't want to hurt you; I *like* you but then ...' I allowed another lull for effect, '... I liked Lily too.'

Alberto's eyelids flickered and the beeping from one of the machines increased slightly. 'Oh yes I lied; I did kill Lily.'

I stood, pushing the chair back as I did so. Leaning over him once more I whispered, 'Remember what I said, Alberto, it's all down to you.' As I bent to kiss his cheek the nurse pulled the curtain back.

'You must leave now dear.'

'Of course,' I gently touched Alberto's hand.

As I turned to leave the nurse walked alongside me, 'I overheard what you said.'

Startled I asked, 'What did you hear?'

'You telling him that it's all down to him. He needs that encouragement.'

I gave a tearful smile, 'I did my best.'

'I'm sure you did.' She laid a hand gently on my arm, 'Have a safe journey back.'

I walked down the corridor and out into the fresh air making my way to the bus stop. I'd done all I could, now it was up to Alberto. Let's hope he can at least get *that* right!

CHAPTER 8

I didn't get back to the flat until well after seven having stopped off at the supermarket to buy a bottle of Malbec and a moussaka and salad, I couldn't face the thought of cooking; the day had proved far more draining than I'd anticipated.

As I stood in the entrance lobby of the flats waiting for the lift – why did it always seem to be on the top floor every time I wanted it – I noticed a slight smell that seemed familiar. Not unpleasant it increased in the confines of the lift. A man's scent like a particularly pungent aftershave. I sniffed a bit harder, it was really rather agreeable but why did it evoke in me a sense of deja vue?

The lift doors opened on my floor and as I let myself into the flat I dismissed it from my mind as the meal and a glass of wine beckoned.

Later, relaxing on the sofa with Liliad by my side I related the events of the day. 'I think Alberto got the message; I can only hope he has the decency to die and save his parents and me more grief.'

Liliad's eyes widened in astonishment.

''Oh no, I didn't mean I was *grieving* for him, I meant 'grief' as in 'trouble' for me. I don't want to be bothering with him now; I want to concentrate on finding my biological father and that isn't going to be easy.'

I knew from conversations I'd overheard growing up in Dorset that, prior to my birth, my mother had worked for a firm of architects in Dorchester. I remembered their name because as a child I'd found it so hysterically funny.

The entrance to Bottomley & Farquhar was situated on the High Street, sandwiched between the chemist and a hardware store. The door opened onto a steep flight of stairs leading to offices that spread over three of the ground floor shop units. I only knew this from what I'd overheard as I'd never been inside the building. In fact I now recalled how, on the few occasions my mother deemed to take me shopping with her, we'd seldom actually passed its entrance, Mother always choosing other routes, other shops to use rather than those on the High Street.

Of course, thirty two years on there was every chance that the firm would no longer be in existence, much less that the same people were still there but it was the only place I could think of to begin my search.

The bus from Bournemouth to Dorchester didn't take long. I settled back in my seat and gave myself up to the scenery and musings. What was my biological father like? Did I resemble him in any way? I definitely had my mother's nose and chin but my colouring wasn't from her my natural hair being a very dark brown. The blonde I now sported was closer to her lighter tones but then, perhaps her hair was dyed; I really couldn't be sure. Mother wasn't tall but she wasn't petite either which I certainly was. Perhaps that came from my father's side of the family; it didn't necessarily mean he was small it could be a throwback gene.

I got off the bus in the town centre and made my way onto the High Street. Some of the shops had changed but not all and although I couldn't locate the hardware store of my memory I did recognise the chemists. The door which I believed had led to the offices of Bottomley & Farquhar was now painted a shiny black (I was sure it had been brown) with a brass plaque alongside stating it was now Henley & Warren, Chartered Accountants.

I shrugged; well I knew I couldn't be *that* lucky, that the firm my mother worked for was still there. I felt quite nonchalant despite the disappointment, probably because the sun was shining with a degree of warmth that suggested winter was finally over and feeling a little peckish I found a café, bought sandwiches and a coffee and took myself over to the town square, found a bench and settled down to eat and consider my next move.

As I took out my mobile and got onto the internet to type in Bottomley & Farquhar I realised I should have done this at home before I set out but, what the heck, it had turned into a lovely day. There was no urgency in my search and even if it proved to be a wild goose chase it wasn't going to matter overly. No, I'd take my time over this, like indulging in a new hobby.

The internet informed me that Bottomley & Farquhar had amalgamated with another architects firm and was now part of Joshua, Laurel and Farquhar (J L & F Ltd) which had offices in Dorchester, Bridport and Weymouth.

Sipping the last of my coffee I ran through the probable time line in my head. Mother had Matt when she was only seventeen; I wondered if that had been an accident too as she would have been five months gone by her wedding date. If that was the case it certainly helped to explain why she and the man I'd believed to be my father seemed so badly suited.

Matt was fifteen years my senior so Mother would have been thirty two when I arrived. I was now thirty two making her, if she'd lived, sixty four which probably meant my biological father was in his sixties or seventies. I couldn't see a much younger man falling for my mother … or could I? The Australian solicitors had sent me a list of my parents' personal effects; I hadn't wanted any of it except a fancy cigarette lighter of my father's and the photograph albums and had passed away several hours in St Joseph's pouring over them. In one respect it had proved a painful experience as there were so very few that included me although that wasn't exactly a surprise.

I thought back to the photographs taken prior to my arrival, when my mother would have been in her mid to late twenties. She really wasn't bad looking; a good figure and delicate features, wide doe-like eyes and I knew she could turn on the charm when she wanted. I'd watched her in action as I grew; at parties and with dinner guests. She certainly wasn't averse to flirting with friends' husbands and by the looks on the wives' faces, with some success.

On reflection it wasn't beyond the realms of possibility that she'd 'pulled' a younger man, say someone in their early twenties so he'd now be in his late fifties – a much more pleasing concept for me.

I stood and walked across the square to the refuse bin and threw away my lunch wrappers. Deciding to follow up my research now I was here I made my way to the newsagents and bought a local town street map. Princes Street, the address of J L & F Ltd wasn't too much of a walk and as the weather was warm with only a light breeze I was happy to stroll around the area, reacquainting myself with the few landmarks I remembered.

Princes Street was part of a business park and J L & F Ltd appeared to occupy about two thirds of a purpose built office block on the left of the street with car parking in front.

The front door opened into a communal lobby with another door and intercoms for the various offices. I pressed J L & F Ltd.

'Hello, can I help you?'

'I'm afraid I don't have an appointment but I wondered if I might have a brief word about your architectural services.'

'Come through, we're the first door on your right.'

The door buzzed open and I walked through into a long corridor that housed ladies and gents cloakrooms plus what looked like a kitchen at the far end. Entering the offices I was greeted by a receptionist, probably in her mid- fifties, sitting behind a large desk that gleamed immaculately in the sunshine that streamed through the window to her left. Behind her was a half-glazed door that led into an open plan area with several personnel sitting behind computers or pouring over drawings laid out on a large central table. The receptionist smiled a welcome.

'Hi, I'm looking for an architect on behalf of my aunt.'

'Well, we've several here to choose from,' she grinned, 'take your pick.'

I grinned back acknowledging her friendly approach. 'I don't need to see anyone at the moment, I just wondered if you had a company brochure I could have a look at.'

'Sure no problem.' She rummaged in the cabinet beside her. 'Here, there's more information on our website.'

'That's perfect, thank you. Have you worked here long?'

'More years than I care to remember. I started with Bottomley & Farquhar straight from school when they were in the High Street.'

'Really, you must be due a gold watch soon!'

'Uh, I don't think so, not with this lot. It was different in the old days; Mr Bottomley was old school, his staff mattered to him but it was a much smaller concern then. Once he retired Mr Farquhar amalgamated the business with Joshua and Laurel.'

'You were lucky to keep your job, weren't you?' I asked sympathetically.

'In a way, yes I was lucky; the receptionist they had got pregnant and left. It was only meant to be temporary to cover her maternity leave but she decided not to return so here I still am.' She spread her hands expansively.

'Well, thanks again for your help. I'll be in touch.'

'You're welcome.'

As I left it occurred to me that this could be a real stroke of luck; she could prove a useful contact but I didn't want to press too soon. I'd go home, read the brochure, peruse the website and decide my next move. I checked my watch; almost three thirty. I should just make the next bus back to Bournemouth.

CHAPTER 9

Standing beside Liliad I followed her gaze to the triangular patch of sea visible in the distance between the houses opposite. For the first time in months the sun was so brilliant that the water's surface glinted like crumpled tinfoil. I gave a contented sigh and laid my hand on Liliad's shoulder. 'Isn't this just perfect?'

Liliad moved her head slightly indicating our ongoing chess game but I wasn't in the mood.

'I think I'm going to take myself for a walk on the beach.' Donning my walking trainers and fleece I slung my handbag over my shoulder. 'I won't be long.'

I weaved my way through the streets deciding to get down onto the beach via the gardens where I'd walked before wanting to see if the warmth was encouraging any more new growth. Taking my time I luxuriated in the warm and gentle breeze coming off the sea and remembering the sensation of being followed that had accompanied my previous walk through these flowerbeds, chided myself once again for my foolishness. How could anything be amiss in this beautiful place? I reached the beach without incident and started to walk along close to the water's edge. If only this was summer; the thought of lounging on the sand and maybe going for a swim; God, I hadn't done that in years. I made a mental note to start looking for a swimming costume.

Walking along, my head down as I looked for interesting shells I didn't notice the young couple coming toward me until their dog, a scruffy but cute looking mongrel, barrelled into my legs. Clambering up, its front paws up to my knees, mouth open in a wide panting grin and tongue lolling to one side it acted as though ecstatically pleased to see me.

'Maxi! Here, now!'

My shock at the voice almost caused me to stumble backward as the dog pushed itself off my legs and bounded back to its owners. For a split second I considered turning on my heels and walking away, my back to the couple but it was too late, they were already upon me.

'I'm *so* sorry,' the young woman apologised, 'I hope he hasn't dirtied you.'

I hung my head down slightly in the hope that my long hair would obscure my face. 'No, it's fine.'

The man was squatting down putting the dog back on its leash. My heart was pumping so hard it set up a rhythmic throbbing just above my left eye. Desperate to get away I took a couple of steps forward just as the man stood upright and turned toward me.

'Maxi's a rescue dog and hasn't had much training but we're working on it.'

I kept walking, turning my head away from him as though looking at the horizon. 'No problem. Bye.'

I didn't dare turn around to see if they were watching me but quickened my pace, desperate to increase the distance. By the time I figured it was safe to stop I'd walked at least half a mile. I found a cluster of large boulders and sat, trying to control the slight trembling in my legs.

How could I be so unlucky? The odds against this happening at all must be enormous but *twice*! I brought my heel back and kicked at the boulder in exasperation and temper. After all these years and all these miles – bloody Barry Mason! I wasn't sure if I was angry with Barry for being there or myself for being so lax. Having seen him in the restaurant I should have been more on my guard. I could only put it down to my relief at being out of the confines of St Joseph's and the soporific effects of living by the sea but either way my lapse of concentration was not only unforgiveable but potentially dangerous.

I took a few deep breaths and forced myself to think logically. I'd first seen him in that Italian restaurant but I felt sure he hadn't recognised me; he'd hardly got a glimpse as I'd hurried into the street, he was too busy picking up the chair I'd knocked over and in any case, I'd kept my face averted and partially covered by my hat.

What about today's encounter? I now looked very different to the woman in the restaurant with my hair dyed and the extensions and also different to the person he'd known all those years ago. In addition his attention had mostly been taken up by the dog so, on balance, I thought I'd got away with it yet the encounter had completely spoilt the day for me. I couldn't relax, my eyes darting everywhere as I walked back. By the time I reached the flat I was in a foul mood.

Dropping onto the sofa I undid my trainers and flung them in temper to the opposite side of the room, knocking over one of the landlord's ornamental vases. 'Oh for God's sake!' The vase broke into three pieces as it hit the wood flooring. I got up and stomped into the kitchen to get a dustpan and brush but catching sight of a half empty bottle of Malbec changed my mind and poured myself a large glass instead.

Returning to the lounge I lay full length on the sofa, the television remote in my hand, ready to switch it on in time for the national news. Liliad sat watching me, a thoughtful expression on her face. I met her eyes but the intensity of her look made me falter and I quickly averted my gaze. I didn't want to tell her about Barry Mason just yet so I turned on the TV instead.

The usual stories filled the room; mindless violence, race hatred and catering to the public's insatiable appetite for details of celebrities sex lives. I'd almost drifted off when the topic changed to the recent crash on the M25.

"It was announced this morning that the young man seriously injured in the recent crash on the M25 near Heathrow Airport died in Hillingdon Hospital late on Tuesday night.
Alberto Jackman was wanted by police in connection with the disappearance of Annalee Theakston, a patient at St Joseph's Psychiatric Hospital in Endover."

A photograph of me taken at my trial flashed onto the screen just as I raised my glass to Liliad. 'Alberto's done something right for once. I must be more persuasive than I thought.'

The commentator continued.

"Miss Theakston was convicted two years ago of the murder of Melissa Hartnell, fiancée of the eminent psychiatrist, Dr Andrew Metcalfe. It was whilst she was receiving treatment at St Joseph's that she went on to kill Dr Metcalfe himself."

The image changed to outside Endover Police Station.

"Detective Chief Inspector Munroe, do you have any information on the whereabouts of Annalee Theakston?"

The interviewer thrust his microphone close to Munroe's face.

"This is very much an ongoing investigation and my colleague, DI Wilson is following up several leads.'

Wilson, standing beside Munroe, inclined his head slightly in acknowledgement. The interviewer turned to Wilson.

'Are your enquiries focussing on any particular area?'

Wilson, not as used to dealing with the media as Munroe and keen to make his mark replied,

> *'Yes, we know Miss Theakston has connections with the Dorset area and …'*

Munroe shot him a venomous look and cut across.

> *'It is important the public, should they have any information regarding her whereabouts, contact us immediately but under no circumstances to approach Miss Theakston. She is a particularly dangerous individual."*

What did he mean by several leads? I slumped back on the sofa; this really wasn't improving my mood. As I turned Liliad to face me I caught sight of my reflection in the dark depths of her eyes. I didn't look anything like the photograph on the news. 'I'm not Annalee Theakston any more, Liliad; I'm Coral Wright.'

Liliad looked at me with an expression that asked, 'Who are you trying to convince, me or you?'

I got up and walked into the bedroom to look at myself in the full length mirror. My blonde hair and extensions did make a huge difference but perhaps I'd better get my eyelashes and eyebrows tinted as well for a complete colour change.

I went into the kitchen and poured another glass of Malbec then returned to the lounge.

'Wilson's certainly been climbing the career ladder, hasn't he?' I commented to Liliad. 'He was a mere Detective Constable when we first knew him; then Detective Sergeant and now an Inspector no less. I bet he'd love to arrest me; it'd be a real feather in his cap.'

I took another sip of wine, appreciating its relaxing effect. Pressing the remote once more I settled back to watch a programme on the life of the Praying Mantis.

CHAPTER 10

The next day I made my early morning life-saving mug of coffee and took it back to bed with me. I wanted to think without Liliad looking at me with what I perceived was disapproval at my lack of progress in finding my biological father. I got the impression that although she clearly enjoyed living in Bournemouth she was uneasy at the prospect of our remaining in one place too long and I had to admit that after the Barry Mason encounters I was inclined to agree with her.

I sat in bed perusing the brochure the receptionist had given me and then logged onto the internet to check out J L & F's website. My difficulty was finding out who, other than Mr Farquhar of the current personnel, had been members of Bottomley & Farquhar all those years ago. Looking at the fresh faces on the website the firm seemed a young and dynamic concern with Mr Farquhar being the oldest and now relegated to the role of consultant. It seemed the only way forward was to chat with the receptionist. My mother had worked at Bottomley and Farquhar since Matt was old enough to go to nursery school, making her about twenty when she started. The receptionist had said she'd been there since leaving school and so would most likely have known my mother.

How to get close enough to the receptionist to start asking searching questions was the problem. I'd have to watch her for a while; find out her habits and routines and then determine my approach.

In the meantime there was Mr Farquhar. Younger than Mr Bottomley as he was still working, albeit in a reduced capacity, he was surely a candidate for my mother's affections. If the photograph in the brochure was anything to go by he must have been quite handsome thirty or so years ago. He still had a good head of thick hair, with somewhat distinguished looking grey flecks at the sides. It was only a head and shoulders shot so I couldn't tell how tall he was but from his face I reckoned he was fairly slim still; he hadn't developed the sagging jowls or broken veined skin of someone overly fond of good dining and fine wines. In fact he struck me as being rather debonair.

I needed to make his acquaintance but outside of the office. Realistically I couldn't trail him and the receptionist; I'd have to employ some help.

◆

I'd chosen a beauty salon and had my eyebrows and lashes tinted a much lighter shade than they naturally were and whilst there decided to have acrylic nails fitted. Along with some multi-coloured wrist bangles I felt more like Coral Wright than ever.

I was still aware of the possibility of bumping into Barry Mason again but my confidence at remaining unrecognisable was increasing with every little change I made. Encouraged by Liliad's gentle prodding I'd located a detective agency positioned at the back of a group of local shops some way from the town centre and had made an appointment for just after lunch.

The entrance door was tightly tucked into the corner made by an L-shaped terrace of one bedroom apartments and apart from its name plaque was no different from all the other entrances to the private residences. The whole area was shabby; litter blew about the yard in front of the buildings, paint on many of the doors was peeling and some of the window cills were clearly rotting. The place appeared deserted, the only noise other than the click of my boot heels was the dull throb and reversing beep, beep of delivery lorries to the shop units in front.

There didn't appear to be a buzzer so I tentatively tried the handle. The door opened onto a set of stairs leading steeply up to a small square landing, the area lit by a single naked bulb that did nothing to dispel the gloom or detract from the threadbare carpet. The only sign of life was a faint tapping as of a keyboard. I took a breath and began to climb. The steps had so little depth that even my small feet had to be placed slightly sideways. With my hands outstretched I let my fingers brush the walls to either side for a modicum of support silently cursing the narrowness and height of my boot heels.

Having reached the landing without mishap there was only one choice, a door to my left which sported a D-shaped static metal handle two-thirds of the way up. I pushed against it, blinking slightly in the glare of an overhead strip light.

At my entrance a young lad paused in his typing, fingers poised a few inches above the keyboard; he didn't look above seventeen. Both dumbfounded by surprise we simply stared at one another for a few seconds before I gathered my wits. 'I'm sorry, I must have the wrong place; I was looking for the Blanchford Detective Agency.'

The young lad stood and extended his hand, 'That's me.'

Shocked, my mouth slightly open in astonishment, I absent-mindedly shook his proffered hand eventually managing to utter, 'There must be some mistake; I need a private investigator.'

The young man bowed very slightly. 'At your service; please take a seat,' and indicated one of the two chairs against the wall behind me.

Obediently I sat, confusion fogging my brain. He came around the desk and took the chair beside me. 'I can see you're a little disconcerted but I assure you I am a private investigator. My name is Martin Blanchford.' Sensing my disbelief he continued. 'OK, I can see you're still doubtful but I've been doing this work for five years now.'

I shook my head.

'Look, what's the problem?'

I swallowed hard and at the risk of being insulting murmured, 'You look too young.'

He sighed. 'I know; I have this baby-faced chubbiness and I'm not very tall but I'm actually twenty six.'

'Really!'

'Yes, really and I've had some very satisfied clients in the past so why don't you just take a chance and tell me what you want.'

I turned away from him and looked around the room trying to decide if I was the victim of an elaborate hoax. Alongside the desk and computer was a filing cabinet, the middle drawer slightly open revealing a number of neatly labelled files, a pin-board on the back wall displayed post-it notes and a bookshelf in the far corner appeared to contain various law books. Turning to my left I noticed for the first time two other doors, both closed.

I looked back at Martin Blanchford, perhaps I'd been hasty. On closer examination he didn't seem quite so ridiculously young; there was a shadow of whiskers pushing through since the morning shave and some lines about the eyes. He was dressed professionally, more like a lawyer not what I'd expected at all my image of a private investigator being based primarily on television depictions. I gave a conciliatory smile, 'I'm sorry, I feel so embarrassed.'

'Don't be; you're not the first and I'm sure you won't be the last. I suppose if I was a woman I'd be flattered.' He grinned, 'Shall we start again? What can I do for you?'

'I'd like you to trace the home address of this man,' I handed him the photograph I'd cut out of the brochure, 'and I'd also like to know how he spends his time when he's not at work; you know, golf course, restaurants, theatre and so forth and family life – if he has one – who they are. He works as a consultant with J L & F, Architects based in Dorchester.'

Martin looked at the photograph. 'That doesn't sound too difficult; are you going to tell me why you want to know?'

I shook my head.

'Fair enough, well I charge a retainer of two hundred pounds paid up front to cover expenses and get things moving. After that it's fifty pounds per hour plus any expenses over the initial two hundred. You OK with that?'

I nodded and opened my bag to count out the cash.

'Can I have contact details for you?'

'Coral Wright; I'll give you my mobile number,' I said as I wrote it out and handed it to him. 'How soon can you start?'

'I've an assignment that's going to keep me busy for the next couple of days but after that I don't see a problem. I should have something for you by the end of next week.'

I stood and we shook hands as he opened the door for me. 'I'll wait to hear. Oh, do you have a business card please?'

'Of course,' he returned to the desk and picked one out from a box balanced on top of the printer. 'If I'm not available at any time you can speak with my secretary, Jenna.'

Noticing my querying look he explained. 'Jenna's off sick, hence my two finger typing efforts. Goodbye, Miss Wright.'

'Goodbye, Mr Blanchford.' I turned and made my way cautiously down the stairs being careful to place my feet sideways as before. Out in the air I briefly wondered if I'd done the right thing; two hundred pounds was a lot of money to hand over without much security but he'd seemed genuine enough. I guess time would tell and at least I could reassure Liliad that I'd taken some decisive action at last. Tomorrow I'd take the bus to Dorchester again and start investigating Mary Jeffreys, the receptionist at J L & F.

The walk back to the flat along the promenade really lifted my spirits and I thanked my stars that I'd been able to rent a flat so close to the sea front especially after the drabness of the area I'd just left. I resolved that wherever Liliad and I lived in future I would ensure it was on the coast; the air, the sounds and smells – I loved it all.

Entering the apartment block lobby I was aware once again of a lingering scent of what I now decided was definitely man's aftershave. It was particularly sharp; pleasantly spicy but not heady. What bothered me was its seeming familiarity and yet I couldn't quite place it. I thought back over the men I'd known. It certainly wasn't DCI Munroe, he simply stank of pipe tobacco and DC Wilson didn't smell of anything other than baby powder! I grinned to myself at the recollection of his baby faced smoothness; I doubted he'd ever had a need for aftershave.

I tried to cast my mind back to my brother, Matt but that was so long ago and I was just a child, I really couldn't recall if he wore any male toiletries at all. My father did but it was a more mellow, lower key kind of scent. What about the male teachers I worked with at the college? The only one I'd ever spent any appreciable time with was

Ben, tutor on the Small Animal and Wildlife course. Oh my God, Barry Mason! Ben had been his main tutor and mentor. That's where I recognised the scent from; Barry had always splashed it on far too liberally, like a lot of teenagers who haven't yet realised that less is often more.

I was so stunned by the revelation that the lift doors opened and closed and I still stood in the lobby unable to move.

'Did you want the lift?' The woman's voice broke in on my thoughts with an abruptness that made me jump.

'What? Oh, no thanks; I'll take the stairs.' So saying I turned and pushed through the doors onto the stairwell leaving the woman watching me with slight bewilderment as she allowed her toddler to press the lift call button.

I climbed the stairs slowly, deliberately turning the possibility over in my mind. Barry can't be staying in this block, can he? I couldn't possibly be that unlucky; it was bad enough that he was in Bournemouth but in *this* apartment block? No, that was beyond the realms of bad luck; a coincidence too far. By the time I reached my floor I'd decided I was being ridiculous. Lots of men must use that aftershave; I was damn sure it wasn't expensive if Barry had worn it as a teenager and in any case, one would expect his tastes to have altered as he got older.

I really must pull myself together and stop being so irrational, it was most unlike me.

CHAPTER 11

Liliad was sitting where she always was, gazing out of the big picture window toward the slice of sea visible between the roof tops opposite, her focus on the far horizon. I dropped my bag on the floor and went to sit beside her. 'I've just got back from the detective agency and he says he should have something for me by the end of the week.' I turned Liliad's head toward me determined to keep her attention. 'You'd have laughed if you'd seen him, he looks *really* young; it was so embarrassing as I couldn't believe he was who he said he was to start with.' I paused, waiting for some reaction which wasn't forthcoming. 'He reminded me of baby-faced DC Wilson – you remember him, don't you, Inspector Munroe's sidekick?'

As I stared into Liliad's eyes my levity of spirit slowly sank as apprehension crept up my spine, tingling like nettle-rash into my scalp. I recalled Wilson, now Detective Inspector Wilson, on the television news programme. He no longer had the baby-faced naivety evident when our paths had crossed all those years earlier. His whole demeanour was now far more self-assured and confident. What was it he'd said in the interview; that they were following up several leads. I couldn't imagine what those might be but then the police were always plagued by hoax calls; supposed sightings given by sad individuals trying to garner vicarious attention. I didn't think I really had much to worry about.

However, I could tell Liliad was concerned and I hadn't even mentioned Barry Mason to her – I figured she'd totally freak out if I did. She was right; however much we both liked living in Bournemouth we couldn't stay. I needed to move things on and swiftly. I must renew contact with J L & F's receptionist and try to get some background to my mother's time with Bottomley & Farquhar.

◆

Next day the bus to Dorchester was pretty much on time. I got off in the town centre and walked as before, positioning myself opposite the offices of J L & F, concealed behind a large tree. I'd timed my arrival for a few minutes before close of office hours; I didn't want to be standing around for ages especially as the sky now threatened rain.

I didn't have to wait long; Mary Jeffreys was out of the door dead on time walking purposefully in the direction of town. I fell in behind her, quite relieved that she almost immediately took out her mobile and chatted animatedly for the whole distance so absorbed in her conversation I don't think she'd have noticed if she'd had an excited chimpanzee chattering and bounding along behind her.

Stopping off at a corner shop she then turned in the direction of a residential area that mainly consisted of what looked like retirement bungalows, entering number twenty two Runnymede.

I hung around for a while but it was difficult to remain inconspicuous in such a neighbourhood. I was sure I could sense some twitching net curtains so deciding I'd better leave before I aroused too much interest I began to walk back the way I'd come.

Back on the main road I'd just turned left toward town when I spotted Mary several metres in front of me. It appeared that Runnymede was a 'U' shape so had two exits both onto the same main road; she must have left in the opposite direction. Good, I was still in with a chance of apparently coming across her by accident.

Trailing some eight metres behind we'd just got back onto the High Street when her mobile rang. She stopped, taking it out of her pocket and putting it to her ear. I couldn't hear what was being said but by the slump of her shoulders I figured it wasn't welcome news. The call finished after only a few minutes and turning back she walked briskly toward me, her head down and anger in her movements. I decided to remain where I was and deliberately let her almost collide with me.

'Oh, sorry,' she barely looked at me as she apologised and took a step sideways, attempting to go around me.

'It's Mary, isn't it, from the architects?' I blocked her way so that she had no choice but to stop and look at me. I held out my hand. 'Coral Wright, I called in to see you the other day … my aunt wanted an architect.'

'Oh, right; yes, I do remember.'

I smiled my friendliest smile. 'You seem harassed – bad day at the office?'

She shifted her bag onto the other shoulder. 'Not easy, no and now my mother has just decided she needs me to get her some milk and bread for her breakfast tomorrow.' She gave an exasperated sigh. 'I've just been round there as well; if she'd told me earlier I could have picked it up before I went.'

'Elderly parents! I know exactly how you feel. Are you going into the supermarket because you've just reminded me that I need to get some milk too. Let me buy you a cup of tea, if you're not in too much of a hurry that is; you do look as though you could do with a break.'

Hesitating only briefly Mary answered, 'Yes, why not. That'd be lovely; waiting a few more minutes won't hurt her.'

The supermarket café wasn't overly busy; we found a table tucked away from the main crowd and settled down with a pot of tea and two 'naughty but nice' cream cakes. 'I figured we could both do with a treat; my elderly aunt would try the patience of a saint and I'm definitely not a saint!'

Mary shrugged off her coat and let it slide down behind her onto the seat. 'Shall I be mother?'

'Please do.'

For a while we were both silent munching through our cakes and sipping tea. Licking her fingers Mary asked, 'So, has you aunt decided what she wants; if she will use J L & F?'

'No, she hasn't. The trouble is she remembers back years ago when she used Bottomley & Farquhar and keeps insisting she wants them. I can't seem to make her understand that firm simply doesn't exist anymore.'

'Difficult although I can sympathise with her; J L & F are a very different breed.'

'Yes, I imagine so. My aunt keeps on about the "personal touch" that the old firm gave her. She keeps on about a young woman who worked there and was particularly helpful and kind to her, a Brenda Theakston. Does that mean anything to you?'

Mary paused; her cup raised half way to her lips. 'Yes, I remember Brenda. She was really nice to me when I first joined straight from school. I remember I was so nervous but she helped me over the first days, made me feel at ease.'

'Did she stay with the firm long?'

'Quite a few years,' Mary gazed toward the ceiling, her brow slightly furrowed as she tried to remember. 'When I started there she'd been there for a few years and already had a child, a young boy, just a toddler; then she went several years and fell pregnant again; I'm not sure it was planned, you know, such a big gap. Yeah, I remember now, we were all really surprised because she left rather abruptly without telling anyone why – it was later she was spotted by one of the lads out in town, heavily pregnant.'

'What was her actual title? I mean, how come my aunt had reason to know her, was she an architect?'

'Oh no, she was Mr B's PA so if he'd done the architectural work for your aunt she probably would have spoken with her quite a lot.'

I grinned, 'To hear my aunt talk it sounds like they made quite a team!'

Mary grinned back, 'A bit more than that if rumours are to be believed.'

'Really!' I leant forward across the table. 'Do tell.'

Mary hesitated for the briefest second. 'Well, it's so many years ago now I can't see it can do any harm.' She leant toward me so close that our noses almost touched and in a stage whisper said, 'It was generally believed that she and Mr B were quite a bit more than just work colleagues and when she was spotted pregnant and having left so suddenly well, you can imagine the rumours.'

'I expect so. Was Mr Bottomley married?'

'Oh yes, happily by all accounts. He's got two lovely children, adults now of course.'

I picked up the teapot. 'Would you like another?'

'Please.'

Mary stirred her tea absent-mindedly, considering. 'You know, despite all the rumours I was never convinced about them having an affair. Mr B was such a gentleman, real "old school" if you know what I mean. Everything was regimented, ordered; not something that would appeal to a young woman. They were very close I admit; well, you are if you're someone's PA, spending all those hours together, working late sometimes. I mean, I'm sure they had the occasional drink together, even lunch sometimes but an affair? I couldn't quite see it myself but then, to leave so abruptly, just because she was pregnant, didn't seem to make sense.' Mary's voice trailed off into her teacup.

Perhaps Mary was right, perhaps all the suspicions were unfounded and mother's affair had nothing to do with Mr Bottomley. I decided to change tack. 'Your Mr Farquhar is still a handsome man, isn't he?'

Mary looked confused.

'From the brochure,' I explained, 'in his photograph he looks very distinguished. I would imagine he was quite something in his younger days.'

'You bet, really good looking. He had all the girls swooning over him…' she snorted derisively, '… for all the good it did them.'

'Why do you say that?'

'He's gay,' Mary looked slightly wistful, 'such a waste.'

I couldn't hide my surprise or indeed my disappointment. I'd really begun to hope that he'd been my mother's lover and therefore my father. Mary misinterpreted my look. 'I didn't mean to offend; sorry.'

'What? Oh no, not at all; just surprised that's all.' I decided to get the conversation back onto a more formal path. 'I don't suppose Mr Bottomley is still working in some private capacity, is he? I've a feeling my aunt only wants to deal with him.'

'I don't think so, he retired some time ago; he must be in his seventies now. I think he spends most of his time playing golf; he was obsessive about it even when at work. When he retired he bought a house near the golf course on millionaire's row.'

'Pardon?'

'Oh, they're not really all millionaires, it's just what it's dubbed locally; it's Goldsmiths Avenue.' Mary huffed, a decided bitterness in her tone. 'A nice life if you can get it.'

'I see.' I paused trying to come up with a plausible reason for asking more questions. 'My aunt is *so* transfixed on using your old firm. I can see her deciding not to go ahead with the work if I can't find some way of mollifying her. Did anyone other than Mr Farquhar from the firm move into J L & F?'

'No-one that's there now; Bottomley & Farquhar was only a small concern; there were only three other staff – other than Brenda and me I mean. There was a young trainee, Jamie but J L & F didn't want him so he got made redundant. David Nigby, he was a senior architect in his late fifties. They did offer him a position but he turned it down. If I remember correctly his wife was quite a high flier, had a good job. I think he ended up taking early retirement and spent his time tending his garden; he died a couple of years ago – heart attack I think.

The only one who moved across was Philip, Philip Maccleson but he left several years ago now, thank goodness.'

'Why do you say that?'

'He just always gave me the creeps; I'm not sure why, he was perfectly sociable but I always felt he was watching me, you know, sort of observing.'

'Where did he go?'

'Up north somewhere, Northumberland I think. Why do you ask?'

I shrugged, 'No reason, just nosey I guess.' I gave a small chuckle, 'A failing of mine.'

Mary smiled back and gave out a long, heart-felt sigh. 'No good, as much as I'd like to stay here I really must get mum's groceries and get them round to her then I can go home and have my dinner.'

I picked up my handbag, 'It's been really nice chatting with you. I'll just get some milk and I'll be off too.'

We shook hands. 'I do hope your aunt makes a decision soon; J L and F would do a good job if you can persuade her.'

'I'll certainly try – for my own sake if not for hers! Bye, Mary.'

'Bye and thanks for the tea and cake.'

'You're very welcome.'

We both headed into the store and went our separate ways down the aisles. I purchased milk I didn't really need and made my way out toward the bus stop; hopefully I wouldn't have to wait too long. There was a lot to think through, all of which I felt an urgency to discuss with Liliad.

CHAPTER 12

Liliad stared resolutely out of the window as I regaled her with the events of the day. 'Mary, the receptionist at J L & F turned out to be a mine of information. She actually knew Mother all those years ago; the only trouble is she's made me a bit doubtful – I think I may have wasted my money getting Martin Blanchford to investigate Mr Farquhar.' I waited for some response, I felt my comment at least deserved a querying look but Liliad didn't move. Peeved I took hold of her arm and forcibly turned her toward me. Her eyes were cold, an ice-tipped silence swelling the space between us; her unspoken accusation hanging heavy in the air.

I squirmed under her gaze, instinctively aware of the reason for her animosity. 'I know, I should have told you;

I'm sorry.' My voice barely above a whisper I couldn't look at her, instead choosing to pluck at a loose thread of fabric on the chair arm. 'I just didn't want to worry you.' It was a pathetic excuse and we both knew it.

My head still bowed I nervously raised my eyes; Liliad's expression was implacable. I tried to swallow but a lump as large as a walnut seemed to lodge in my throat.

My head buzzed like a wasps' nest; I couldn't lose Liliad's support. She'd been my constant companion for years, letting me talk, helping me plan and silently giving the reassurances I needed. Each time I looked into those huge liquid eyes I instinctively knew if I was on the right path.

'I've seen him twice.' Slowly I raised my head and was rewarded with a miniscule softening of her eyes. 'Once in a restaurant, the first day we arrived in Bournemouth and then when I was walking on the beach; he was with some girl and a dog.' I couldn't bring myself to mention the scent of aftershave in the apartments' lift; such a tenuous thread was bordering on paranoia and I knew Liliad would regard that as weakness.

'I'm certain he didn't recognise me; I look *so* different now and it's so many years since he's seen me but I know I must be careful in future. I mean, I knew I'd have to be alert to the police sniffing around especially in Dorchester but Barry Mason never occurred to me. Lily had said he was returning to Sheffield.' I gave an exasperated sigh, 'It's so unfair!'

I got up and wandered through into the kitchen deciding a coffee and biscuits might raise my mood. Returning to the lounge I was pleased to note that Liliad's features were more relaxed and welcoming. Gently I picked her up and placed her on the sofa, settling down beside her my legs tucked under me. Dunking my biscuit in my coffee I took a mouthful allowing my mind to return to the topic of my search for my biological father.

'According to Mary Jeffreys, Mr Farquhar is gay so not much chance of him being my father,' I paused, considering, 'although I suppose he could swing both ways. Mm, maybe I'll let the detective agent continue his investigations just in case; I'd quite like him to be my father, he's very handsome.' Liliad raised her eyes heavenward in silent vexation, a provocation I chose to ignore.

'Then there's Mr Bottomley; Mary didn't give much credence to my mother having had an affair with him but then she did seem to put him on a bit of a pedestal so her opinion might not be worth much. She reckons he'd be in his seventies by now which is a bit disappointing. Still, worth pursuing, there isn't much else to go on. I need to find out his home address; Mary says he lives in the posh part of Dorchester, near the golf course and plays all the time. It's certainly worth a look around there.'

Just at that moment my mobile rang. 'Ms Wright, Martin Blanchford here, I've got the information you asked for. Do you have an email address I can send it to or would you like to call in some time tomorrow.'

'I can call in tomorrow afternoon, about two if that's OK.'

'That'd be fine; I won't be here I'm afraid but my secretary, Jenna will be. I'll leave the paperwork with her. There's no additional cost, the information you requested was relatively easy to acquire.'

I smiled as I put the phone down. 'You see, Liliad, some real progress at last.'

I took the bus into the centre of town then walked to the detective agency, struck again by the contrast of the area to where my flat was. The location seemed to go downhill with the terrain; even the group of shops behind which the agency was positioned looked neglected and certainly didn't cater for the upper end of the market. A couple of saver shops, a chippy, a mini-mart and a newsagent seemed to be the main requirements of the local population along with a betting shop and a pub. The sooner I was out of the area the better.

Hurrying up to the agency door I pushed against it, nearly bumping my nose when it didn't open. Oh great!

I looked around the yard but the place was as deserted as before. I banged my fist against the wood causing an echo that rippled around the block before fading into silence. Walking across to sit on a low wall I took out my phone to ring the agency number. I tried the office first but got no response. There was also a mobile number, I tried that.

'Martin Blanchford.'

'Mr Blanchford, it's Coral Wright. I'm outside your office but there doesn't appear to be anyone here.'

'Really? Perhaps Jenna's taking a late lunch. If you don't mind hanging around for a bit I'll try giving her a ring.'

Fuming at his casual attitude I replied, 'I haven't got a lot of choice, have I?'

The twenty minutes I waited felt like two hours but eventually I heard hurried footsteps as a young woman rounded the corner gasping out an apology. 'I'm *so* sorry; Martin didn't tell me you were coming.'

I rose and turned toward her, the shock of recognition stopping the breath in my throat. Continuing to walk forward to the door, her head down fumbling for the keys in her handbag she didn't look at me. I fell in behind her, carefully negotiating the stairs in the dim light. In contrast Jenna twinkle-toed up the steps like a ballerina. Unlocking the door into the office she turned and, talking to the top of my head commented, 'It gets easier with practise.'

I followed her into the office as she picked a large brown envelope off her desk and turned toward me. ''Oh, it's you!' She smiled warmly as she held out the envelope. 'I'm really sorry about our dog on the beach the other day. I do hope he didn't mess your clothes up. He's a sweetie really but a bit boisterous.'

I took the envelope muttering 'No harm done,' and immediately turned to leave.

'Can I get you a coffee or tea, to make up for the wait?'

It was obvious she was desperate for some company; she probably spent quite a few hours working alone when Martin was out on assignments. I hesitated, did I really need some banal chitchat with Barry Mason's girlfriend but then again she didn't know who I was so maybe it would be wise to see what I could find out. 'OK, that would be great.' Once again I took one of the chairs by the wall as she fussed over mugs and kettle. 'How long have you been living in Bournemouth?'

'Not long; we came down from Sheffield just for a holiday initially but then with the summer coming we just didn't want to go back. Barry, my boyfriend, is a bit of a gypsy; he'd really like to keep moving. How do you like your coffee?'

'White, no sugar – but you're working so are you intending to stay for longer now?'

Jenna handed me a mug and perched on the edge of her desk facing me, 'For a bit, yes; we're saving up to buy a camper van and then I guess we'll just keep moving, like itinerant labourers, picking up jobs to earn money as we go.' She giggled the prospect obviously appealing to her. 'How about you, have you lived here long?'

'A few months, I'm just getting settled in my flat. Are you renting? I expect it gets quite busy during the holiday season.'

Jenna nodded, 'I expect so but we're OK for now; we're in a static caravan on a farmer's field in the village of Haine, just outside Bournemouth.'

'That's a long way from the shops and here to work isn't it?'

'Yeah but there's a bus that goes past the entrance to the farm so it's not so bad and the farmer lets Barry use an old van so he always picks me up from work and we give Maxi a run on the beach and then go back. It works well and in any case Barry likes being out in the country, the more isolated the better; he's not really a people person.'

'That must be hard for you,' I ventured.

'It's not too bad, we've got Maxi for company and I work here three days a week and in the Nag's Head in Haine Monday and Friday nights so I get the company I need.'

'The Nag's Head, I don't think I know that pub.'

'I'm not surprised, it's mainly just locals from the village but it's close to the farm so ideal for me.'

I dug a little deeper. 'So what does your boyfriend do while you're working?'

'He helps out on the farm with the animals mainly; he's got qualifications in animal husbandry.'

I smiled, 'Well, it sounds as though neither of you will have too much trouble earning a living while you're travelling.' I finished my drink and laid the mug on the work surface. 'Thanks for the coffee but I really must be off now. Good luck with everything.'

'Thanks, you too.'

As I negotiated my way down those lethal stairs I smiled inwardly. Living that far out of town I shouldn't have to worry too much about coming across Barry Mason especially as now I knew his routine and in time they would be gone for good. Still it would be unwise to get too complacent; I knew I must still keep my wits about me.

◆

Entering the flat I shoved a supermarket ready meal into the oven, poured a glass of Chablis and settled into the chair by the window opposite Liliad to peruse Martin Blanchford's papers. I didn't mention my encounter with Jenna, I figured Liliad would only become unnecessarily alarmed and I needed her on side for some time yet; I didn't want her pressurising me to leave Bournemouth and my search before I was ready.

Martin Blanchford had done a thorough job setting out details of Mr Farquhar's home address which, joy of joys, was in Bournemouth. Details of his working for J L & F as a consultant I already knew but what I didn't know was that the closing down of Bottomley & Farquhar and amalgamation with J L & F had been an acrimonious affair, hence Mr Bottomley's early retirement.

The report went on to state that Mr Farquhar had no family but lived with a David Rheinhard as a gay couple and had done so for a number of years although, looking at the dates, not for the time he'd been a business partner with Mr Bottomley.

It seemed he was something of a fitness fanatic having a membership at the local gym where he frequently played squash, swum and used various gym equipment. He and his partner, David enjoyed meals out, the theatre and avante garde cinema. He drove a soft top Lexus, occasionally crewed a sailing yacht that belonged to a friend of a friend and all in all was a good time guy.

I liked him more and more but unfortunately, there was no mention of any women in his life. Nonetheless I wasn't going to give up on him just yet; if there was any chance of him being my father I didn't want to let it go.

Martin's notes stated that he regularly attended the gym on a Thursday evening. 'Well, Liliad, it looks like I'm going on a fitness drive – at least for a short while.'

Thursday evening was only a day away so I'd made a hasty trip to the shops to buy some trainers and gym gear; quite a spend for what I hoped would be a short time but I figured to turn up in unsuitable attire wouldn't endear me to a man of Mr Farquhar's refined, expensive tastes. I wasn't thinking to seduce him, that would have been most inappropriate but I hoped he'd be appreciative of beauty in the world, the friendly sort, in touch with his feminine side.

I arrived at the gym just after seven thirty in the evening which was, according to Martin's notes, when Mr Farquhar had a regularly booked gym session. I signed up for a three month trial membership and then asked to be shown round the facilities. Having done the squash, tennis and badminton courts, pool and spa we eventually got to the gym. It was busy, a lot of the equipment in use. With only half an ear on what the member of staff was explaining I searched the room.

Mr Farquhar was working out on a rowing machine. I felt a surge of physical attraction, totally inappropriate considering the situation but I knew exactly what Mary Jeffreys had meant when she'd commented, 'What a waste.'

I noted there was an unoccupied rowing machine alongside that on which Mr Farquhar was working out so asked my guide if I could have an introductory session on using it. He readily complied. As I settled myself on the seat I made a point of catching Mr Farquhar's eye and gave a warm smile which he acknowledged with a brief nod, not even breaking his rhythm.

I listened attentively to my instructor and began to row. Although it was on the lowest setting I could feel my muscles screaming in protest; I'd never done anything like this in my life! After a few repetitions I insisted I'd got the hang of it and would like to continue for a while, effectively dismissing my guide with the promise to book an introductory lesson for all the other equipment when I returned.

By the time I'd managed another fifteen repetitions I felt in serious need of oxygen and the paramedics. Deliberately clambering off the machine on the side of Mr Farquhar I tried to stand. My ears buzzed with the drone of a gigantic bumble bee, the room a blurred carousel of spinning equipment. I could feel my legs liquefy as I slumped, none too elegantly into Mr Farquhar's arms. His voice sounded as though he was speaking through a wodge of cotton wool. 'I think you may have overdone it, my dear.' He guided me to a chair by the wall. 'I'll get some help.'

'No, please, I'll be fine in a minute. Could you just get me a glass of water?'

He hesitated just a moment before walking over to the water cooler. The room was slowly returning to normal; I sat perfectly still willing the moment to pass. Draining the cup he handed me I murmured my thanks. 'I think I'm just a bit dehydrated; I've been rushing about this afternoon and haven't had time to drink much.'

'Ah, not a wise move; can you stand now? I think a mug of sweet tea might be a good idea. If you like I'll walk you down to the café.'

I looked up into the palest amber eyes flecked with soft gold that sparkled with good humour and was momentarily confounded by an emotional response that was quite unlike me. I mentally shook my head; it must be a reaction from my faint; I needed to get a grip.

I nodded and pushed myself up from the chair. Mr Farquhar gently took hold of my arm and half guided me out and down the stairs to the café. Sitting me at a table he went to the counter and ordered two teas carrying them back with a handful of sugar sachets.

'I don't take sugar.'

'You do now,' he said as he tore open the first packet and poured it into my tea. I watched in silence as he emptied two more sachets into the mug and stirred before sliding it across the table towards me. 'Drink.'

Obediently I raised the cup to my lips; at the first sip I thought I'd be sick it was so sweet but under his authorative gaze I managed to drink about half before he allowed me to stop.

'Feeling a little better?' he asked, his voice sliding over me like honey.

'Yes, lots; thank you.'

'Do you have far to go home?'

'The other side of town but it's OK, I can get a bus.'

Concern flitted across his face,'I don't think you should be standing around waiting for buses; it's almost nine o'clock and getting quite cold. If you can wait while I shower and change, I'll drive you home.'

'Oh, I've been enough trouble already.' I gave a weak smile in apology.

'Nonsense, it's no problem. Wait there, I won't be long.'

I watched as he walked toward the exit, his long, finely toned legs exhibiting an even tan which I didn't think had come from hours lounging on a sun bed; more likely a result of the sailing and active lifestyle outlined in Martin's report. Forcing myself to stop my pleasurable musings I closed my eyes and took a few deep breaths, composing myself. Hearing the door swing open I turned and gave Mr Farquhar my most grateful smile as he waited for me to join him.

Sitting in the Lexus beside him I discreetly studied his profile. He was indeed a very handsome man; clean shaven, his features seemed to have been crafted by the angels; a sensuous mouth below an aquiline nose and eyes that crinkled seductively at the corners every time he smiled. His hair was still thick and expertly cut, a peppering of grey at the edges simply confirmed the impression that this was a distinguished and elegant man.

I knew what I was looking for; that there were features that I could equate to my own appearance.

'You're very quiet; are you sure you're feeling alright?' The faint touch of his breath as he turned toward me caressed my ear, his voice laced with genuine concern.

'Yes, honestly – I think I'm more embarrassed than anything.'

He smiled. 'How long have you lived in Bournemouth?'

I shifted slightly on the seat, taking a few seconds to decide how much personal information to divulge. 'Only a short while; how about you?'

'I've lived here most of my life, mainly in Dorchester where I worked but now that I'm only part-time I decided I'd prefer to spend my golden years in Bournemouth.'

'What work do you do?'

'I'm an architect – a consultant now, just a couple of days a week.' He pulled over to the side of the road. 'Is it alright if I drop you here?'

'Yes, that's perfect. It's really very kind of you; you must let me buy you a coffee sometime as a thank you.'

'No need, it's been a pleasure. Take care.'

I stood on the pavement and watched as the car pulled away, my whole being yearning for this man to be my father.

◆

Entering the flat I made the excuse to Liliad that I was really tired and just needed a bath and my bed. Thankfully she didn't object or create a fuss so I escaped to the solitude of the bathroom. Soaking in the warm scented water I closed my eyes and gave myself up to my imaginings. To know Mr Farquhar was my biological father would be icing on the cake; it didn't matter to me that he was now openly gay; what mattered was that I felt this was a father of whom I could be proud.

There was just one slight niggle that persisted, like an itch I couldn't quite scratch. Martin Blanchford's report had stated that the closure of Bottomley & Farquhar and the amalgamation with J L & F had been acrimonious; I wanted to know why.

CHAPTER 14

Hobbling into the bathroom the next morning, the muscles in my legs screaming in protest, I vowed *never, ever* to spend another minute on a damn rowing machine. I recalled a notice I'd once seen in a shop, "I love fitness – it's the exercise I can't stand." My current physical state gave me no reason to disagree.

After a hot shower I felt slightly more human as I made my way into the kitchen for coffee and toast. Taking it through into the lounge I opened the curtains and sat in the chair beside Liliad, looking out at the slice of sea that we were beginning to regard as our own.

Liliad looked at me enquiringly. I finished my breakfast and updated her on my meeting with Mr Farquhar. 'It was *so* embarrassing; I genuinely did almost faint, it wasn't an act but as it turned out it was for the best because it got me closer and for longer than I think I'd have been able to manage otherwise.' I paused, thinking back over the evening. 'He really is a lovely man and I'm sure I can see a likeness between us.'

Liliad's eyes widened slightly, scepticism evident in her look.

'His nose is similar to mine and his hair was really dark once and thick like mine.' I tugged at one of my lengthy blonde locks, 'Well, like mine naturally is, I mean.'

Liliad's eyes shifted once more to look out at the sea and the far horizon.

'Yes, I know I've got to speed things up and I am. I'm going to start investigating Mr Bottomley tomorrow but I've decided I can't keep travelling to Dorchester every day so I'm going to find a pub that has rooms and book in for a while; that should speed things along a bit. I know it means leaving you behind again but if I don't get anything definite within the next three weeks we'll leave the area – I promise.'

I glanced down at the chess board on the window cill, some pieces seemed to have moved since we last played with my queen potentially under threat. I looked at Liliad who met my eyes, looked down at the board then back at me. I hesitated, my hand hovering over the pieces but deciding I didn't have time just now I went to get my coat.

Trying to find my biological father was becoming not so much a relaxed hobby as an obsession. My desire to find out who I truly was overriding every other consideration.

◆

The bus trip to Dorchester was beginning to become monotonous; I was doing it so often even the bus driver started to recognise me. 'You again,' he commented as I boarded. I merely smiled in response wanting to make as little impression as possible.

Alighting once more in the High Street I waited around for the little local bus that would take me out toward the golf course. Leaning against the wall of the bus shelter I was enjoying my favourite pastime of people watching when a police car cruised past, travelling excessively slowly as though looking for someone. I withdrew further into the shelter, shuffling along the back until I'd managed to tuck myself behind an overly large man who was also waiting. As the police car moved on I realised I was holding my breath and let it out in one long sigh. The man in front turned toward me, 'That was heartfelt,' he smiled in friendship.

'Just tired,' I replied.

'Ah, here it is; after you.' He stepped aside to let me go in front of him. I walked to the back of the bus taking a seat by the window on the driver's side. We were just passing the chemist's and entrance door to what had once been Bottomley & Farquhar's offices when I glimpsed a form that caused my heart to pump blood into my stomach like a lead weight. I swung round to look out of the back window as we pulled away – DI Wilson – absolutely no doubt about it. I slumped back in the seat, my mind in overdrive. It took a few moments before I could calm myself enough to think logically.

It was only what I'd expected and what Liliad had feared. With DCI Munroe's knowledge of my family history and DI Wilson's comments during his TV interview it was reasonable to assume that my childhood area of Dorset would be at least a partial focus of the police search for me. I'd made light of Munroe's revelation about my parentage but he might well suspect that curiosity would get the better of me. I recalled that I'd asked him if my mother had divulged who her lover had been; on reflection that was a mistake as it exposed my desire to know.

Liliad was right, I needed to move things on quickly or give up my quest and melt away. The possibility of a return to St Joseph's was anathema to us both.

Lost in my thoughts I almost missed my stop, frantically pressing the bell as we sailed past. Fortunately the driver was the accommodating sort and restricted himself to commenting that it'd be better if I gave him more warning next time. I apologised profusely and hurried down the step.

On the pavement I took stock of my surroundings. Mary Jeffrey's was right, this was an affluent area. All the houses I could see were detached, many double-fronted with double garages and room to park at least three other cars on the forecourt without detracting from the large front gardens. The avenue culminated in a T-junction; to the right heading back towards town and to the left the entrance to the golf course.

I had no idea which house was Bottomley's so had decided to make discreet enquiries at the golf club. From the type of cars in the car park it was obvious this was a members' only club, the fees of which dictated the exclusivity of its members. Daimlers, a Rolls Royce, Lexus, Jaguars and BMW's – the whole collection spoke of wealth and prestige. I didn't think for one moment that any request I made to become a member was going to be even remotely entertained so I needed to find another excuse for sullying their doorstep.

The club bar and restaurant was approached through the golf shop staffed by one young man behind the counter and another tidying shelves. I approached with a deliberate air of obsequious humility. 'Good afternoon, I'm sorry to bother you but I've an important message for Mr George Bottomley from his wife. She says he's playing here this afternoon but that his mobile is always switched off so she's asked me to walk down and get a message to him. The problem is, I don't know what he looks like.' I gave a small apologetic smile, 'I've only ever met his wife,' I offered as explanation with a slight shrug of my shoulders.

The young man behind the counter tapped something into his keyboard, gazing at the computer screen for a few seconds he replied, 'Yes, he tee'd off at one thirty,' he looked at his watch, 'three o'clock, he should be about half way round by now. If you go outside and turn left he should be coming up to hole nine. After that they have to cross the path to get onto the second half of the course. He's in a group of four.'

'OK, how will I recognise him?'

The man stacking shelves turned toward me a wide grin splitting his face, 'You won't miss George Bottomley; he's the one wearing the plus fours.'

'You're kidding me.'

'No, our George is a stickler for the old ways; thinks everything should be steeped in tradition.'

'Well, thank you both very much.'

'Pop back in if you have a problem,' the counter man offered, 'and I'll send someone out to get him.'

I turned and left the shop keeping everything crossed that they were correct and I wouldn't miss him. I needn't have worried; just as I was leaving the car parking area I spotted a group of four golfers crossing over to hole ten. A squat, portly man with a loud, booming voice was holding court, his remote controlled electric trolley coasting along in front of him as he used his free hands to gesticulate in the air, obviously elaborating some point that his companions appeared to be ignoring – not that that was holding him back. He looked absurd; checked plus fours in some sort of tweed looking fabric topped with a sleeveless diamond patterned multi-coloured sweater and long sleeved white shirt and tie. Woollen knee high socks finished the ensemble.

I couldn't believe anyone so ridiculous could be my father; he certainly wasn't the kind of man I could imagine my mother falling for. Briefly I wondered if he was even worth bothering about; if he *was* my father I'd really rather not know. Mr Farquhar was a much pleasanter proposition but then I recalled Martin Blanchford's report that the split at Bottomley & Farquhar wasn't amicable. It felt like a loose end and I didn't like loose ends; they always held the possibility of tying you up in knots later.

I figured this group would be on the golf course for at least another two hours then there'd be the inevitable dissection of the game in the clubhouse afterwards. I reckoned I'd got at least another three to four hours before Mr Bottomley headed home. I'd noticed a café a couple of bus stops before I'd alighted, I'd walk back there, have some lunch and then return.

I hoped to follow Mr Bottomley and see which house he lived in. There were only half a dozen detached houses on Goldsmiths Avenue so even if he was lazy enough to drive to the course I should still be able to stand at the top of the road and see which house front he pulled into.

◆

Warm and bright, the café was more of a chintzy tearoom with prices to match but I couldn't fault the bowl of homemade vegetable soup, crusty artisan bread followed by a pot of tea and an enormous slice of Victoria sandwich cake. I ended up feeling decidedly mellow and totally stuffed so the last thing I wanted to do was stand around near the golf club to check out George Bottomley but needs must; what with DI Wilson hanging around Dorchester and Barry Mason in Bournemouth I was beginning to realise that Liliad was right and time was of the essence.

Figuring I'd look less conspicuous by the bus stop I checked my watch every five minutes, time crawling by like a constipated sloth. By five thirty the sun had retreated and there was a decided nip in the air. I wrapped by coat closer around me and walked a little way toward the entrance to the club simply to pass some time. Turning back towards the bus stop the Rolls Royce I'd noticed in the car park glided past me so silently it could have been hovering a few inches above the tarmac. Indicating right it turned into Goldsmiths Avenue. I quickened my pace so that I was at the T-junction just in time to see it turn into number three. I sauntered down the avenue on the opposite side coming abreast of number three as Mr Bottomley was hauling his golf clubs out of the boot.

As he walked toward the house the front door opened and a slight, diminutive woman pressed herself against the wall of the lobby as she held the door back to allow Mr Bottomley and his golf bag entrance.

'Move yourself, Muriel; I need to put the clubs there.'

The woman made a slight bop like a half curtsey and scuttled deeper into the hallway. 'Did you have a good game, dear?'

I didn't catch Mr Bottomley's reply as the door firmly closed behind him. I checked my watch, ten minutes to the next bus into town and the room I'd booked at the George and Dragon pub.

CHAPTER 15

The George and Dragon was a pub of two halves; a modern open-plan bar and restaurant area was tacked onto a much older lounge bar over which ten en-suite bedrooms were situated. The incongruity struck me when I was handed my room key, one for a deadlock that wouldn't have been out of place hanging from the belt of a keeper in the Tower of London.

Feeling slightly chilled from an afternoon of standing around in the cold I settled down to the traditional fayre of steak and ale pie, mash and mushy peas; far too much considering what I'd eaten in the café that afternoon but delicious nonetheless. Two large glasses of Pinot Noir later and I was finding it difficult to negotiate the stairs to my room; my slightly inebriated state not being helped by the undulating floor of the narrow corridor the outside wall of which leant inwards so that even I, at five foot three, was in danger of cracking my skull.

The door to my room didn't seem square to the wall either. As I placed the key in the lock and turned it gave a metallic clunk that resonated along the hall. I pushed on the door and stumbled over the threshold, nearly falling onto the double bed that was only two steps away from the entrance.

Pushing the door shut I locked it with the key and shot the bolt that was also present. It didn't seem that being accosted during the night was something I needed to be concerned about. I dragged myself onto the bed and waited for the room to stop moving. There was another door at the foot of the bed. Eventually I sat up, placed my feet on the floor and with deliberate care made my way toward the second door. It opened onto a small bathroom with a delightful deep, claw-footed free-standing bath – bliss!

I turned on the bath taps and then ran the cold water in the sink; fortunately it was really cold so I filled a glass and drank twice to dilute the red wine in an attempt to stave off a headache and the dry mouth that was becoming quite unpleasant. Sliding into the bath I luxuriated in the warm water feeling it ease my aches and calm my mind. Tomorrow I would tackle Mrs Bottomley.

◆

A bright sun and warm breeze made the short bus ride to Goldsmiths Avenue a pleasure. I'd left my visit until the afternoon reasoning that Mr Bottomley, in view of Mary Jeffreys' comments, was a man of habit with a routine from which he seldom strayed but just to be on the safe side I walked up to the golf course first. Yes, his Rolls Royce was in the car park so I should be safe for a couple of hours at least.

I strolled back to number three Goldsmiths Avenue running tactics over in my mind. From my brief glimpse of Mrs Bottomley I figured she was the nervous type, easily disconcerted. I needed to keep her calm so a friendly, non-threatening manner was called for.

As I approached the front door I took a notepad and pen from my bag and adopted an air of friendly professionalism. The bell, as I pressed it, gave out the sonorous bongs of a large church bell; I could guess that was one of Mr Bottomley's choices.

The door into the porch from the house opened and I found myself looking into the anxious eyes of a woman barely my own height giving a pale imitation of Lady Macbeth by the persistent wringing of her hands. I produced my brightest smile holding up a business card I'd purloined from the George and Dragon pub which I briefly flashed before her, sliding it back into my pocket before she had any chance to read it.

'Hello, Mrs Bottomley, I apologise for disturbing you; my firm has been commissioned to conduct a survey into the closing down or amalgamation of private architectural firms and I wonder if I might ask you a few questions. It won't take long.'

Mrs Bottomley glanced nervously to either side of me as though she was expecting someone to emerge from the bushes. 'You'd need to speak with my husband about that; I don't know anything about the business.'

'Ah, now that's just the point; what we're interested in are the personalities involved; the psychology behind the decision not the dry business facts. We're talking to the wives of partners of small sized firms because we believe they play a crucial role in any successful business even if that role is seldom acknowledged.'

Mrs Bottomley hesitated, her hand hovering over the handle of the porch door.

'May I please come in? I promise I'll only take up a few minutes of your time.'

She took a deep breath and continuing her unintentional Lady Macbeth impression screwed "her courage to the sticking place" and opened the porch door. 'Do you mind coming through into the conservatory; it's more cheerful in there.'

I followed her down a long gloomy hall and into the kitchen from which patio doors opened out into a large, curved conservatory giving views the length of an immaculate garden; a profusion of crocuses, daffodils and jonquils asserting that spring was definitely here in earnest.

'Gosh, what a lovely garden – is it your doing?'

Mrs Bottomley smiled in gratitude. 'Yes, it is.'

'Did you design it too or was that Mr Bottomley?'

Mrs Bottomley took a sharp intake of breath and pulled herself up to her full, rather lacking, height. 'No, Mr Bottomley has nothing to do with the garden; he tries to direct my work from the patio but I pretend I can't hear him.'

I gave Mrs Bottomley a silent round of applause acknowledging her small act of rebellion.

'Would you like a cup of tea?'

'That would be very welcome, thank you.' I settled myself into a chair in the conservatory, placing my notebook and pen on my lap.

'If I could just make sure I've got a few facts straight first, Mrs Bottomley…'

Amid the chink of fine china Mrs Bottomley called, 'Please, call me Muriel.'

'Muriel, from the information I've been given I understand the firm of Bottomley & Farquhar consisted of Mr Bottomley and Mr Farquhar as equal partners; a senior architect, David Nigby; a draftsman, Philip Maccleson and a trainee, Jamie …er, oh dear, I can't read my own writing.'

'Jamie Johnson,' Muriel supplied.

'Ah yes, I can see it is now. Also there was a PA, Brenda Theakston and a receptionist, Mary Jeffreys. Is that it?'

'Yes that's correct.' Muriel carried in a tray holding the most delicate bone china cups together with a plate of Belgian chocolate biscuits.

'Gosh, you're spoiling me,' I grinned as she held the plate up for me to choose.

'Why not; while the cat's away.' Muriel gave a slight snigger as she bit into one of the larger biscuits in the selection. Perhaps she wasn't quite as cowed as at first appeared.

'Perhaps you can give me a little bit of history; how did your husband and Mr Farquhar meet?'

'At the rugby club; George used to play when he was younger; he'd been a member for quite a few years when Tony Farquhar joined the team. I think he'd just moved into the area. Anyway George had been wanting to set up in practice on his own but felt he wouldn't make enough income alone so was looking for someone to work with him and then hopefully buy into a partnership at a later date. Tony came along at just the right time and the business slowly grew from there.' Muriel sipped her tea then reached across for another biscuit.

'So when did they enter into a partnership?'

'Oh, I don't know; about five years later I think. Tony was a real asset and by then they'd grown the firm to a reasonable size. I think Tony had been left some money when his parents died so he had the capital then to buy in.'

Muriel seemed to be transforming before my eyes, her carapace of timidity cracking wide open. I got the impression that she didn't often get the chance to have her voice listened to. If I played this carefully I could open the flood gates.

'I still don't understand why you want to speak with me, you can get all this information from my husband. Would you like some more tea?'

'Yes please.' I handed my cup across. 'Thank you. The thing is, Muriel we've discovered that if we just talk to the business partners we get all the financial and commercial reasons for any decisions but never anything to do with the psychology of the reasoning behind those decisions. It's seldom the case that personalities didn't have at least some bearing. Women are much more attuned to these things, even wives who haven't been directly involved with the firm. There aren't many husbands who don't talk about their work issues over a bottle of wine and a good dinner.'

Muriel reached across for another biscuit. 'I see; well yes, George did often talk about the office over dinner.' Brushing some chocolate coated crumbs from her lips she added, 'It's about all he ever did talk to me about.'

I smiled, 'Well, you know what they say, "Behind every successful man is an exhausted woman."'

Muriel nodded, 'Amen to that.'

'So when it came to the decision to amalgamate with Joshua & Laurel was it a joint decision; did Mr Bottomley want to retire at that time anyway?'

Muriel stretched out her hand for another biscuit but then thought better of it, placing her hands in her lap instead. Concentrating on fiddling with her fingernails she kept her head lowered so that she didn't have to meet my eyes, an embarrassed awkwardness in her manner. 'It was all very uncomfortable at the time; you see, George had absolutely no idea; I sometimes wonder if he even realised such people existed; when he was faced with the reality he just couldn't deal with it let alone *accept it.*'

'Accept what?'

Shifting uncomfortably on her seat Muriel finally lifted her head to look at me. 'That Tony Farquhar was gay, a homosexual. George was horrified, it was against everything he believed in; how he thought a man should be; against his religion; against his whole sense of common decency. To continue working together when he'd found out was simply out of the question as far as he was concerned.'

'How did he find out?'

'One evening; he'd been home for a while when he realised he'd left some papers in the office that he'd wanted to go through that night so he went back and he found them, Tony Farquhar and Philip Maccleson.' Muriel gazed abstractedly out toward the garden. 'It was all rather sordid.'

'Oh dear, I see; how very unpleasant for everyone.'

'Yes it was. I did try to smooth things over; make him understand that, you know, in this day and age … but it was no good. He was furious with me for even suggesting he should let it go; he said one of those "perverts" in the office was enough but to discover he had *two*! He determined to dissolve the partnership, conducted all negotiations through his solicitors; he wouldn't even speak with Tony. He insisted on a very good financial settlement to buy his silence so that Tony could put whatever spin on the closing of the firm he wanted so it wouldn't hinder him getting another position – hence the eventual amalgamation with Joshua & Laurel.' Muriel continued to stare at the garden. 'He only did that to save face himself; there was nothing charitable about it.' She stood up, a lightness in her movements. 'Do you know that's the only time I've ever spoken of it to anyone; it's really quite a relief. I wanted to contact Tony, tell him how sorry I felt about everything; he was a genuinely nice man … but I daren't … if it ever got back …' She shook her head slightly as if to dispel the unpleasantness, 'Let me refresh this tea,' and before I could reply she'd picked up the tray and carried it through to the kitchen.

'May I stroll round the garden?'

'Yes, please do.'

I could hear the kettle heating as Muriel rinsed out the cups. What I'd learnt this afternoon was a huge disappointment as it made it almost certain that Tony Farquhar couldn't be my father. As for Mr Bottomley, God forbid! It was true that I couldn't envisage my mother having an affair with such a bigoted prude but I needed to get some degree of confirmation.

Muriel joined me as I gazed into the depths of her kidney-shaped lily pond. 'Tea's ready.'

We turned back toward the conservatory as I asked, 'Do you think Mr Bottomley's PA, what was her name, Brenda, knew any of what was going on; I understand she worked for him for quite a few years.'

Muriel considered for a moment. 'No, I don't think so. She knew Tony and Philip obviously but she'd left the firm a few years before this all happened. I remember George was quite lost for a while without her; she'd been an excellent PA – well, according to George – I never met her.'

'Did she go to another firm?'

'No, she had a teenage son and we discovered after she'd left that she was expecting again although she didn't say at the time. She did leave rather abruptly as I recall; didn't work a notice or anything; George never could understand why but I expect she'd just had enough of him; he's not the easiest of people to get along with.'

I smiled, 'Yes, PA's do tend to grow rather close to their bosses. I read somewhere once that it was like being married but without the sex.'

Muriel giggled, 'Well, she wouldn't have got any of that with George – far too straight-laced! To be honest, I think theirs was a genuine friendship more than anything else; a definite fondness on both sides. George was somewhat protective of her. He once said that he didn't think she had a particularly happy marriage; she was so young when her son was born. I don't think things were very easy.'

Muriel looked thoughtful for a few moments and as if talking to herself said quietly, 'George wasn't always so brusque; I think Brenda leaving so suddenly without any explanation and then the business with Tony, well, it shattered his faith in human nature. He felt he'd supported them both just to be let down – sad really.'

It took me another half an hour to extricate myself, Muriel obviously starved for company and conversation.

'Will any of this get back to my husband, any report or anything?'

'Not if you don't want it to; in any case, everything will be anonymous – we won't name names.'

Muriel visibly relaxed, 'Good, he'd be livid if he knew. He's a very private man.'

I thanked her again and smiled my goodbye leaving with the salutary lesson that one should never rely on first impressions; Muriel Bottomley was not a timid inconsequential mouse after all.

CHAPTER 16

Having caught the local bus back to the town centre I hurried to catch my connecting bus to Bournemouth; I didn't want to linger in Dorchester, the sighting of DI Wilson uppermost in my mind. My thoughts drifted towards DCI Munroe, I couldn't believe he'd relinquished the whole of the investigation into my disappearance over to Wilson; things were far too personal for that. If nothing else I was sure he'd be hovering in the background somewhere, lingering like a bad smell on the edges of my life. Liliad was correct, we really couldn't afford to stay in the area for much longer.

By the time the bus pulled into Bournemouth the breeze had dropped and a late afternoon sun lingered, its gentle warmth like a lover's embrace encouraging me to stay outside for a while longer. I decided to walk through the gardens that led down to the promenade. Plucking off a sprig of rosemary as I passed I held it to my nose and inhaled its delicious scent. Rosemary for remembrance – I thought of Lily with fondness. When I'd told Alberto she'd been my friend I'd spoken the truth. Her death had been my loss as well as Munroe's but it was a price I'd been willing to pay.

I found a vacant bench amongst the flower beds and sat, the smell of turned earth pronouncing the abundance of organic life within as I breathed air deep into my lungs, gazing out toward a sea as still as a millpond; its surface a shimmering metallic brilliance of reflected light.

I needed to think, to assimilate all the information I'd garnered from Mrs Bottomley that afternoon before I spoke with Liliad.

I was now convinced that Mr Farquhar couldn't be my father, as regrettable as that was and Mr Bottomley was, I was sure, a non-starter. I'd decided at the outset that I was interested in tracing my biological father only if it meant I could make contact, form a relationship with him. As Mary Jeffreys had told me that the senior architect, David Nigby had died I wasn't going to waste time pursuing that line of enquiry. In any case, I figured he really would have been too old for my mother to have formed a roman- tic attachment. At the other end of the scale was Jamie

Johnson, the trainee but I couldn't see my mother being a cradle snatcher either. There was only one possibility, Philip Maccleson but according to Mrs Bottomley he was as gay as Tony Farquhar. To crown it all I had to acknowledge that it was quite possible my mother had lied, or my father had misunderstood or indeed, DCI Munroe had lied. My whole quest could be a complete non-starter.

I sighed deeply as I directed my gaze toward the horizon, a slight chill passing over me as the brightness of the sun was momentarily obscured. Turning to pick up my jacket from the bench surprise pinned me to the seat with the force of an electric shock.

'Hello again.'

Barry Mason was sitting on the other end of the bench. I hadn't even sensed anyone there. Dumbfounded I merely stared at him as he continued. 'You're quite safe; I've left him at home.'

I opened and shut my mouth but no words came out.

'Maxi, my dog,' he said in explanation.

At last I managed to emit an almost unintelligible acknowledgement as I hastily gathered my jacket to me.

'Don't leave on my account, please; I didn't mean to startle you.'

'It's alright, I was just leaving anyway; I have to get back.'

'Ah, obviously a busy lady.' He lolled back on the bench, his long legs stretched out in front of him in a posture so reminiscent of those long ago college days. He paused as I took a couple of steps away from him. 'Strange the way we keep bumping into each other; Jenna said she'd met you too, the other day, where she works.'

The annoyance was obviously evident in my expression as he quickly back-tracked, 'She didn't tell me anything; Jenna's much too professional for that. She only said she'd met you again and that you were really nice about having to wait for her to get back from lunch.' Sensing my anger he continued, 'You won't make a complaint will you? Jenna needs that job.'

I turned and faced him directly figuring that if he knew who I really was now was as good a time as any to find out. He didn't betray a glimmer of recognition. 'No, of course I won't make a complaint. Goodbye,' I said firmly and turned away, walking swiftly down to the promenade. I needed to get back to the flat; I needed to talk to Liliad.

◆

Back home I poured myself an overly large glass of Shiraz and sat in the chair opposite Liliad, my hands slightly trembling despite my concerted effort to hide how unsettled I felt. Liliad's eyes fixed on my face unwaveringly, locking me into her stare; all I could see was my reflection, a pale doll suspended in the liquid depths of her eyes.

Knowing that Liliad wasn't going to like what I had to report I swallowed, trying to shift the lump of apprehension in my throat. 'Things haven't gone as well as we might have hoped.' Liliad's head tilted slightly to one side enquiringly, waiting patiently for me to continue.

'It seems certain that Mr Farquhar and Mr Bottomley are non-starters as far as being my father is concerned. Realistically there's only one option left, a Philip Maccleson. He worked at the firm at the same time as my mother and moved over when they amalgamated. He'd be in his fifties now.'

I decided not to mention Philip's association with Tony Farquhar; I didn't want to give Liliad any reason to object to my trying to trace him. 'Mary Jeffreys told me he'd moved away to Northumberland so I'd need to employ a private investigator again … another one.'

Liliad blinked just once, a silent demand for an explanation.

'I just think it's better to spread myself as thinly as I can so no-one gets to learn too much about me.'

Not giving Liliad a chance to question me any further I rose and walked through into the kitchen to pour another glass of Shiraz. I didn't like telling Liliad half-truths, it sometimes felt as though she could look into my soul, my deception obvious to her. Also, I knew that I'd put us both at risk over this venture; for our own safety I should have just left it alone, melted away somewhere remote where we had no previous connections. Instead we had the potential threat of Barry Mason and, although I hadn't told Liliad, the police were sniffing around too. Yet I couldn't let it go.

I wanted to know why he'd abandoned me as he so obviously had. Maybe if he'd stuck around my life could have been quite different. Also, as Inspector Munroe had enjoyed pointing out, I wasn't who I'd thought I was; the past thirty two years had been wiped away by his revelation. I needed to confront this man; I needed answers.

I sat on the sofa my legs stretched out along its length and considered my next move. I needed Philip Maccleson traced, if that led nowhere I would give up once and for all but until then … I glanced across at Liliad; she was staring out of the window again her back toward me like a physical barrier between us. I toyed with the idea of going across, picking up her strings and dancing around the room with her; anything to lighten her mood and dispel the stain of the atmosphere between us but her stiff, unyielding posture made it plain that such an approach would be forcefully rebuffed. Instead I turned on my phone and surfed the internet to find a detective agency outside Bournemouth.

I'd been looking for about five minutes when a thought struck me; perhaps Tony Farquhar knew where Philip

Maccleson was. From what Mrs Bottomley had told me they'd obviously been close once, a situation that hadn't changed when the firm amalgamated as Philip had moved across with them so one would assume that Tony Farquhar had pulled a few strings. Mr Farquhar was now with a new partner; I wondered if that was a consequence of Philip leaving or had been the cause of his relocation to Northumberland. Either way it was possible Mr Farquhar knew something of what had happened to Philip but I didn't feel I could contact him direct.

Dragging myself off the sofa I went to the sideboard and pulled out the envelope containing Martin Blanchford's report. Scanning the pages I found what I was looking for, Tony Farquhar's address in Bournemouth. He worked Tuesdays and Thursdays and I knew was at the gym every Thursday evening so it seemed that Thursday would be the best time for me to approach his partner.

Tony Farquhar's home was a three-storey modern town house with a balcony jutting out from the second floor accessed by sliding glass doors that I assumed led off the lounge; a sort of upside down property with probably a kitchen and dining room on the lower floor and bedrooms in the roof space. It looked out over the gardens and promenade to an uninterrupted vista of the sea. It must have cost a fortune! A slope led down to a double garage the doors of which were open in readiness for Mr Farquhar's Lexus to return. Empty except for a couple of ladders, a tool kit and two expensive looking mountain bikes chained and padlocked to the wall it exuded a neatness suggestive of obsessive compulsive disorder.

I walked back and forth in front of the property a couple of times to reassure myself it was unlikely that Mr Farquhar was at home and then walked up the steps to the front door and pushed the bell. It gave out a melodious chime that I was sure was from Bach's harpsichord concerto; the contrast to Mr Bottomley's clanging announcement couldn't have been more pronounced.

A couple of minutes passed before I heard the click of steps on tiles and the door opened. David Rheinhard stood before me modelling a pair of yellow rubber gloves, a vinyl apron displaying a buxom form barely covered by a skimpy bra and panties and brandishing a toilet brush. I was so surprised I almost dropped the bottle of wine I was carrying as I choked out, 'Is Mr Farquhar at home?'

Seemingly unperturbed by my reaction David Rheinhard wafted the toilet brush heavenward as though conducting an angelic choir, 'No, he isn't; can I help?'

'I wanted to give him this,' I held up the bottle of wine, 'as a thank you for his help last week.'

David put out his free gloved hand as if to take the bottle from me but then thought better of it. 'Whoops, better not; not exactly hygienic. Why don't you come in for a minute; I've almost finished the bathroom spring clean.'

I followed him down a gleaming black and white tiled hallway. A large Persian cat sat motionless in the centre of a black square, its long silver grey hair glinting in the sunshine that filtered through the latticed window. As I approached I bent down intending to stroke its head.

'I wouldn't,' David advised, 'Crystal's not the friendliest of cats.'

I immediately withdrew my hand as the cat poured itself, in one fluid movement, over the tiles like a chess piece rolling out of place; its green eyes fixed on me with a venomous stare.

David opened a door to his left. 'If you wouldn't mind waiting in the kitchen for a minute I'll just finish what I was doing and get out of this elegant attire.' He indicated the apron, 'The pinny is my sister's idea of a joke so I get my own back by only wearing it for the most unpleasant of jobs.' He grinned as he held the toilet brush aloft and left me to wait.

I placed the bottle of wine on a surface and wandered around the kitchen; it was as immaculate as everything else I'd seen and fitted out with every gadget one could wish for. A notice board affixed to the back wall was festooned with reminder notes, a shopping list and business cards for a plumber and an electrician. The fridge freezer seemed to have been reserved for a display of postcards, held in place by a variety of cryptic magnets.

'Those are Tony's.' David entered the room so quietly I hadn't heard him approach. 'Can I get you a coffee?'

'Please, that would be lovely.' I pointed to one of the postcards, 'That looks familiar, where is it?'

He glanced across at the one I was pointing to, 'Lindisfarne; Holy Island.'

'Of course it is, I should have recognised it. Are they all from Northumberland?'

'Mostly; Tony has a friend up there, an ex-work colleague. How do you like your coffee?'

'White, no sugar.' I turned to look at the postcards again, 'Do *you* like the Northumberland coast?'

'No, it can be a bit chilly for me.' He handed me my coffee as he continued, 'I don't know why Tony still keeps them; he has very little contact these days.' He indicated the bottle of wine standing on the work surface. 'You didn't say why you felt you owed Tony a thank you.'

I smiled ruefully, 'It's a bit embarrassing; I met him at the gym last week, well, I actually fell into his arms, quite literally. I overdid the exercise and came over faint. He was really kind, bought me a mug of tea and even drove me home.'

David nodded, 'That sounds like Tony, always helping people out.'

Just then the house phone rang. 'Excuse me a moment.' David put down his coffee and walked out into the hall.

While he was gone I seized the opportunity to examine a couple of the postcards taking them down from the fridge. One was a cryptic message simply stating that any delay would have consequences; the other was more interesting. Apparently the writer was considering purchasing a cottage just over the border into Scotland at a place called St Maabs. Both were simply signed 'P'. I just had time to replace the cards before David returned.

'Sorry about that,' he indicated the hall phone call.

'No problem; I need to be going anyway; thanks for the coffee.'

As we walked down the hall David asked, 'Did Tony tell you his address?'

'Not exactly; I told him that I had just a glimpse of a sliver of sea from my flat and he then said how lucky he was to have such a fabulous view overlooking the gardens as well as the promenade so I did a bit of sleuthing and figured it had to be in this block somewhere. I tried about three other houses in the row before I struck gold.'

David seemed satisfied with this explanation merely commenting, 'Yes, we are lucky here.'

The cat was once more on the same square of tile as we walked to the front door, its eyes scrutinising me. I noticed it flexed its paws as I passed, extending needle-like claws. I shuddered slightly feeling as vulnerable as a mouse pinioned to the floor.

CHAPTER 17

I walked down to the promenade through the gardens and onto the beach feeling lightness in my spirit. My talk with David Rheinhard had proved productive in that I was convinced the 'work colleague' Tony Farquhar was in touch with in Northumberland was almost certainly Philip Maccleson. Why the relationship should continue all these years and at such a distance I couldn't fathom but whatever it was it didn't appear to bother Tony's current partner.

Liliad would be pleased for it would get us well away to an area where I had no previous connections and hopefully it would see an end to my search one way or the other. The thing now was to get back to the flat and start making plans to leave but first I wanted to pop into the town centre and get something for dinner. I headed off the beach and back onto the promenade then took one of the main roads towards the supermarket.

Leaving with my bag full of goodies – I couldn't resist treating myself to a large chocolate caramel bar and yet another bottle of wine – I took a short cut down a narrow alleyway toward my flat. It was straight for approximately eight metres before taking a right turn so acute that it formed a completely blind bend.

My arms wrapped around my bag of groceries as I clutched it to my chest I walked swiftly, my head down as my mind grappled with the practicalities of getting Liliad and I to Northumberland. As I turned the corner I smacked into a man coming the opposite way with such force I stumbled backwards on impact, the wind knocked out of me.

'Well hello again, *Miss Thompson.*'

I looked up into eyes that held the scrutiny of a cold beam of light. Barry Mason towered over me, his six foot frame so threatening that I contracted into myself, in-stinctively creating as small a target as possible. My mind numbed with shock we stared at one another in silence for a few seconds before I managed to utter, 'You're mistaken; that's not my name.'

Barry's mouth broke into an oily, sibylline smile, 'Of course it isn't; for now.'

I considered turning back and making a run for it but knew I'd never outpace those long legs and deeply feared turning my back on him. Instead, I opted for bravado, taking a couple of steps towards him as I responded, 'I don't know what you're talking about. Let me pass.'

Barry planted his feet more firmly on the ground as I moved and stretched out his arms in an imitation of Da Vinci's anatomical drawing of Man, placing his hands on the walls either side, effectively blocking my way. 'I think you and I need a long talk.'

I eyed him coolly, the shock of our impact replaced by a calm confidence at dealing with this novice. 'I have nothing to say to you.'

'But I have a lot to say to you and you would do well to listen.'

Just at that moment we both heard footsteps in the alley behind me. Barry reached down and in one smooth movement plucked the groceries out of my hands and took hold of my arm, propelling me forward just as a young mother and toddler turned the corner. I could do nothing but go along with him as he chatted away about inconsequentials as though we were a couple just finished the weekly shop. The grip of his fingers on my upper arm was painful as he guided me out of the alley and over to a bench on the edge of the car park, forcefully causing me to sit, positioning himself against me and placing my groceries to his other side.

'Well, Miss Thompson, a lot has happened since our college days hasn't it?'

I inflected some anger into my voice, refusing to be cowed. 'Will you *please* stop calling me that, it isn't my name.'

Barry smiled, 'No, I know it isn't; it wasn't your real name all those years ago in college and now you're calling yourself Coral Wright; not that that's your name either, is it?'

I sneered, 'Oh, so Jenna isn't as 'professional' as you claimed.'

'Good God, no, much too much of a chatterbox is my Jenna and very useful it's been.' He picked up a lock of hair from my shoulder and flicked it slightly between his fingers. 'I must say, the hair does make a huge difference to your appearance but it's the eyes that betray you.'

I slapped his hand, extricating my hair and turned my head away as he continued; the smugness of his tone nauseating. 'I think of those college days with a degree of fondness.' He gave a slight chuckle. 'Do you remember when I asked you for some extra help with my work; a little one to one private tutorial session. You were so naïve it was pitiful; my mates dared me to try it on with the delectable Miss Amelia Thompson but I wasn't lying when I said you had the most beautiful eyes; you do, quite striking; I've never forgotten them.' He paused. I was finding it difficult to breathe, the air between us suffocating as though he was sucking all the oxygen out of it. He lowered his voice and leant in a fraction closer toward me, spitting his words in my ear. 'Just as I've never forgotten the hell you put me through.'

Slowly I turned to face him, it was clear my calm, unruffled response was undermining his confidence. Unblinking I looked directly into his eyes. 'I'm listening.'

He shifted slightly on the bench, an indication he wasn't as confident as he pretended; a chink in his armour. 'I always wondered why you'd taken such an interest in me at college; I was only in your class as a 'filler' subject; you knew I didn't have the slightest interest in art history but when my father died in suspicious circumstances you were all over me; offering me advice, giving the police misleading information to keep them off my back. I've realised since that you even engineered my meeting Lily Munroe.' He paused, looking inwards, reflecting. 'She was a truly sweet person; she didn't deserve *you*.' His bitterness was corrosive.

He moved slightly so that his body was turned toward me and he could look directly into my face. I didn't turn away but matched him look for look.

'Lily getting accidentally shot in the police raid on my cottage was dreadful but it was later when her dad and I went over what we both knew that your manipulation of events became apparent but then, you ended up in that psychiatric hospital. Lily was so certain that you were sick, that you didn't mean for any of it to happen and I figured maybe you'd had your punishment being in there. I never thought they'd be stupid enough to let you out so you could get your claws into Lily again.'

I kept my expression as blank as the effigy on a stone shrine.

'Lily and I split up; everything that had happened had all been too much and in any case her dad still couldn't accept me … just not good enough for his precious princess … but then, you know all that don't you?'

I said nothing; I wasn't going to help him through this.

He took a deep breath as though he'd got through the worst of his memories and continued, his tone lighter, more at ease. 'I went back up to Sheffield, got a job in an animal sanctuary but I kept in touch with Mrs Munroe. She'd never felt about me the way her husband did; she kept me up to date with everything about Lily and you. She'd believed, like Lily, that you were just ill but when Lily died on that mountain in Scotland she started to doubt and when Lily's camera was found with those final photographs … Of course, nothing could be proved, you weren't actually on any of the photos, just an arm, but she knew and so did Inspector Munroe – he just couldn't prove it.'

'Fascinating but as you say, no proof.'

Barry carried on as though I hadn't spoken. 'You must know the police are looking for you; it'd be so easy for me to point them in your direction but I figure you owe me. I don't know why you're in Bournemouth or why you employed a PI to look into some chap's life and I don't care. Jenna and I want to travel, buy a big camper van and hit the road so I thought, what better way for you to make amends for all you've put me through.'

At last we'd got to the nub of the matter and as always, money was determining the path to be taken. I sat absolutely still, looking hard into those heavily lashed dark eyes. I wouldn't plead lack of money, I wouldn't grovel; I'd played the game far too long to be outdone by a novice. Keeping my voice steady I responded, 'I don't have that amount of money readily available; you'll have to wait until I can cash in my premium bonds and some shares, probably a couple of weeks.'

Barry shrugged, so sure of himself. 'OK, Jenna's got to give two weeks' notice at her job; that should fit in just fine.' He hoisted my grocery bag onto my lap and stood in front of me. 'I shall be watching you so don't think about doing a vanishing act.'

I watched as he sauntered across the car park; despite the intervening years he was still the same cocky little oik I'd known at college. He may think he'd progressed from a pawn to a knight but a knight's moves are limited whereas a queen can cover the whole board in a single move.

CHAPTER 18

I walked slowly back to the flat going over in my mind the conversation with Barry, the unsaid threads of which formed knots in my mind. He could easily change his mind and notify the police of my whereabouts; I wondered again whether he'd been in my apartment block, that lingering scent of aftershave still bothered me but I hadn't noticed it today and he'd sat close enough to me, I could hardly have missed it so possibly just a coincidence. Either way it didn't seem that getting me locked up again was his priority, once he'd got the money maybe but not before.

He'd said he'd be watching me; well, he couldn't watch me every hour of every day. I thought back to my chat with Jenna; she'd said she worked in the pub Monday and

Friday nights so Monday seemed as good a day as any; the sooner the better.

Entering the flat I found Liliad in her usual place gazing out to sea, one hand laying lightly on a chess piece as though frozen in mid-move. I sat opposite, 'Gosh, it's warm in here,' I leant across to open the window, 'was it your move next or mine, I forget.'

Liliad's head turned very slightly toward me just as her hand knocked over her king, a sign that she'd relinquished the game. Confused I looked at the board; when we'd last played she had my queen under threat; there was no reason for her to throw the game. Perhaps it was an accident, a draught from the open window causing her arm to move. I reached across intending to right the piece so the game could continue but Liliad's hand shifted slightly again, covering her king while her eyes widened, a penetrating stare directed at me. 'OK, so you don't want to continue the game, that's fine.' I walked through into the kitchen and poured a glass of Sauvignon Blanc, glad that I'd bought it on my trip to the supermarket.

I waited a while before returning to the lounge, considering. It was clear Liliad just wanted away from here and this frostiness would continue until I complied. Telling her about Barry wouldn't help matters; I decided to only let her know what I'd found out from Tony Farquhar's partner and of my plans to move us to Northumberland.

I would go to the bank tomorrow, Friday and close my safe deposit box so all my money was to hand. It wouldn't matter if Barry was watching me, he knew I'd have to get my monies together so my going to the bank wouldn't be particularly suspicious.

On Monday I would buy a one way train ticket to Berwick-on-Tweed to leave very early Tuesday morning. I'd go to the station late on Monday afternoon when I knew Barry would be meeting Jenna from work and walking their dog so couldn't watch me then, Monday night, I would deal with Barry Mason once and for all.

◆

Over the weekend I removed my hair extensions and dyed my hair black; my natural hair was just long enough now to gather in a grip at the nape of my neck. I removed the acrylic nails I'd indulged in at the beauty salon and cleansed all the make-up from my face. I stayed indoors the whole weekend packing our few belongings, which really didn't amount to much. I wasn't going to give Barry Mason anything to watch.

By late evening on Monday all was in place. I donned my tracksuit bottoms and hooded jacket, wrapped a large piece of cloth around the can of lighter fuel I'd purchased and shoved them into a pocket before catching the last bus from Bournemouth to Haine.

Haine was more of a hamlet than a village, a small general store and the Nags Head pub being the only services I could find. The entrance to the farm was easy to find for, as Jenna had said, the bus stopped right outside. There didn't seem to be anyone about so I walked towards the pub veering off into a wooded copse just before so that I could hide but see people coming and going. About seven o'clock Jenna arrived to start her shift, she'd walked so I knew it couldn't be far from the caravan in which they were living. I waited another half an hour and then walked back to the farm entrance.

Cautiously I made my way up the lane listening intently for the sound of any human activity, ready to push my way through the hedgerow to hide in the field if necessary but all was quiet. It was nearly eight o'clock and night was closing in. I switched on the torch facility on my mobile phone, I wasn't used to the countryside; I hadn't realised how inky black it could be. Tree branches spread out across the fading night sky like the tortured arms of the dead; there were indistinguishable rustlings in the hedges on either side and disembodied cries rent the air, my hearing so acute that the scrunch of my feet on the gravel was amplified tenfold.

What the hell did I think I was doing? If I didn't spot the caravan in the next five minutes I'd leave. Then I heard it – music; someone was playing an acoustic guitar. I headed toward the sound and there, just inside the field entrance was a very old mobile home, the sort of mainly hardboard and plywood construction, lights ablaze inside.

I turned off my torch, the light from the windows being enough to make out general shapes. There was something leant against the building covered with a tartan blanket. I crept close and pulled up the covering. Two bales of hay, obviously from last year's harvest, were apparently being used as outside seating. Perfect, I wouldn't need the lighter fuel and cloth after all which made it less likely that arson would be suspected.

I cut the string on one bale so I could pull a couple of wedges apart. Kneeling down I shoved them under the caravan. I took out my father's lighter and was flicking the lever trying to get it to ignite when I registered that the music had stopped. I could hear and feel the vibration of footsteps as someone moved about inside. As the door opened sending a shaft of light across the field I squirmed under the building and lay motionless.

'OK Maxi, out you go and hurry up.'

The dog bounded down the steps as the door slammed shut. Within a couple of minutes Maxi was under the building with me, tail wagging exuberantly as he licked my face and used my prone body as a trampoline, jump-ing on and off. 'Maxi, get off!' I hissed as I pushed him away but it was as though he was on a piece of elastic, he just kept bouncing back like it was all a huge game. In desperation I flicked the lighter again, this time I got a flame and as Maxi came toward me I thrust the flame at his nose. He gave a loud yelp of shock and pain and shot out into the night.

A couple of seconds later the caravan door opened again and Barry came down the steps calling out for Maxi; he must have heard the yelp. I lay still, hardly daring to breathe and watched as Barry's feet walked the length of the caravan and back again. He kept calling for Maxi until eventually I heard him say, 'There you are, you daft mutt. What's the matter?' He crouched down so low that had he turned in my direction I'm sure he'd have seen where I was huddled. However, his attention solely taken up with the dog, he examined it closely. 'What the hell have you been poking your nose into this time? Come on inside, let's see what I can do about it.' Picking Maxi up, he retraced his steps, the door closing with a resounding bang behind him.

I waited a couple of minutes more then hurriedly lit the wedges of hay, wriggled back out and set light to the bales leaning against the caravan. Then, pulling up the hood of my jacket I raced out of the field and down the lane toward the main road and the Nags Head.

Moving round the side of the pub I leant against the wall getting my breath under control after my run. Pulling out my mobile I called for a taxi. 'Be there in about fifteen minutes.'

'Thanks, that's fine.' I wandered around to the pub's deserted back garden and sat on a bench, the darkness effectively shielding me from being noticed. Leaning back I watched, fascinated, as sparks illuminated the night sky followed by an explosion. I supposed it must be the calor gas cylinder. Amid clouds of smoke a cerise glow coloured the sky; it really was quite beautiful.

Immediately after the explosion the pub emptied, its clientele dashing off to see if they could help, just before my taxi arrived. 'Looks like some fire,' my driver commented, 'probably a hay stack too tight and too wet; can make it overheat.'

'Really,' I settled into the back seat, 'I didn't know that. Bournemouth please, Edward Manse Road.'

'Right you are, luv.'

Next morning I laid Liliad very carefully inside the suitcase fashioning my cashmere sweater into a pillow for her head and carefully positioning her strings down either side of her body so there was little chance of them tangling on route. 'I'm sorry you've got to travel hidden again but I daren't take the risk of drawing attention to myself and you always attract *so* much attention.' I stroked her cheek as I stared down into her wide, clear eyes; the irises as green as ivy looked back at me, the pupils dilated and black as pitch, holding my reflection in their viscous depths. Liliad held my gaze for a minute then slowly closed her lids, her dark brown lashes resting softly against high cheek bones.

We were catching the seven fifteen morning train to Berwick upon Tweed, partly to leave Bournemouth as early as possible but also because on this train we only had to change once, at Birmingham. The last thing I wanted was to have to go into London and out again; the further I could keep away from my old area the better.

The postcard I'd read in Tony Farquhar's home had mentioned buying a cottage in St Maabs; according to the map the nearest town to that small enclave was Berwick upon Tweed, hence my decision to stay there initially. St Maabs looked so tiny I knew I'd probably stick out like a sore thumb if I just turned up outside the holiday season. I wouldn't have to wait long for more visitors to be about as we were nearly into May and so far the weather had been exceptionally clement, hopefully encouraging an early start to peoples' holidays.

Although the journey took just under eight hours it seemed to pass relatively quickly – at least for me; I doubt Liliad felt quite the same entombed in the suitcase so I'd resolved to find a B & B as close to the station as possible in order to end her incarceration as soon as I could.

The B & B I settled on was definitely past its heyday, a fact reflected in the price but it was clean and tidy albeit somewhat jaded. Still, I couldn't be picky, my funds were becoming stretched, soon I would need to find some seasonal work or Liliad and I would find ourselves sleeping on a park bench.

The owner, Mr Warren, as tattered as his establishment, shuffled ahead of me up the wide staircase. In his mid-sixties, presenting a professional appearance wasn't top of his priority list. I couldn't help noticing the threadbare elbows of his brown cardigan and the shiny seat of his trousers as I followed him up the stairs. I smiled to myself as some lines of T S Eliot came to mind, "I grow old … I grow old … I shall wear the bottoms of my trousers rolled." However he was enough of a gentleman to insist on carrying my case for me.

Reaching the landing we turned right down a narrow corridor, its plaster walls painted deep beige, scuff marks evident at the lower level. The uneven floor prevented any chance of a wheeled suitcase being dragged in a straight line. I wondered how Liliad was faring as my case bashed against the wall a couple of times. We passed four doors before we came to what appeared to be a dead end. A large window looked out onto the main street and beside it a concealed hallway, just wide enough for one person at a time led off to its left with a door at the far end, like a private entrance.

Mr Warren preceded me, entering the room and propping my suitcase against the double bed, he then stood to one side to allow me access into what turned out to be a spacious room with views across the town square. Breathing heavily from the exertion he handed me the keys, one to the room and one to the main entrance door. 'The front door's always locked but you can come and go as you please. Breakfast is seven to eight thirty downstairs, if you miss it, you miss it – we don't provide any alternatives so don't go asking for room service.'

He moved toward a door in the far corner of the room, dragging his feet across the carpet as though to lift them an inch above the floor was too much effort. Opening the door with a flourish he explained, 'This is your en suite shower room.'

I peered into the tiniest en suite I'd ever seen; I calculated I could sit on the toilet, wash my hands in the basin and my feet in the shower all at the same time. Noticing my perplexed look he continued somewhat grumpily, 'If you want a bath there's a communal bathroom down the corridor but you need to give the tank an hour to heat up. How long are you planning on staying?'

'About a fortnight.'

He didn't reply, just gave a brief nod of acknowledgement and left.

I locked the door behind him and carefully lifted the case onto the bed. Unzipping it I sighed with relief to see that Liliad's position had barely altered despite her rather rough ride along the corridor. Lifting her out, I settled her on the bed plumping up the pillows behind her. Her head turned immediately toward the window. 'No sea view I'm afraid but there's plenty to watch.' I snuggled up beside her. 'I'm not planning on being here for long; I intend to move us up to St Maabs because that's where the postcard was from. The cards were signed simply 'P' and Tony's partner said it was an old work colleague so it's reasonable to assume its Philip Maccleson. He's the only one of the old firm of Bottomley & Farquhar who I haven't yet found out much about. He moved across when the firms amalgamated and was in the old firm for quite a few years, including while my mother was there so he's definitely of interest. I know that according to Mrs Bottomley he had the relationship with Tony but it doesn't exclude him as a possible candidate for my father; maybe he's bisexual.' I paused, considering. 'I wonder why he left R L & F. His relationship with Tony continued until David Rheinhard came on the scene so maybe that's why he moved all the way up here.'

Liliad's expression said it all; maybe, maybe, maybe … very tenuous but all I had to go on.

I left Liliad sitting on the bed, locking the door behind me as I went. I really didn't think Mr Warren would be the sort to pry, he was much more inclined to have as little to do with his guests as possible; that suited me fine. Once out in the street I headed toward the town centre to find a newsagent. I bought a street map – my sense of direction is hopeless so without it I'd probably be unable to find my way back to the B & B – then entered the first estate agents I encountered. 'Good afternoon, do you deal with any property sales in St Maabs?'

The woman behind the desk smiled a welcome, 'Not really, they don't come up very often. Please, take a seat.' She indicated the chair my side of the desk. 'Were you looking for anything in particular? Does it have to be St Maabs?'

'Yes, it does, I have my heart set on it.'

She got up and walked to a filing cabinet, pulling open the top drawer and flicking through some folders. She was about my own age, in her early thirties but a little overweight I thought and she really shouldn't wear her skirt so short, not with those legs! I glanced down at my tracksuit trousers, badly crumpled and stretched out of shape at the knee due to all those hours sitting in the train and decided that perhaps I really wasn't in a position to criticise someone else's appearance. I smiled warmly as she turned back toward me.

'No, we don't seem to have anything at present. Most of the cottages in St Maabs are holiday lets; you'd be better speaking with Brown and Wilson on Connaught Road, they deal with the holiday market and sometimes handle longer term lets and, I believe, the occasional sale.'

'OK, thanks I'll give them a try.'

I stepped outside and consulted my map; Connaught Road wasn't too far away. I looked at my watch; four thirty; they'd probably be closing soon but if I hurry … I arrived just as they were closing the door. Damn! I'd have to come back tomorrow.

There was a small park opposite; I wandered across and plonked onto a bench, suddenly aware of how very tired I felt. I was also hungry, realising I hadn't eaten properly since breakfast. I'd have to find somewhere to eat before I returned to the B & B; Mr Warren had made it crystal clear that not even a sandwich would be on offer there.

I found an Italian restaurant and ordered spaghetti Bolognese and a large glass of Merlot. I always find pasta dishes so satisfying especially when I'm famished and a little chilled. I hadn't thought about it being so much colder here than in the south and my wardrobe was seriously depleted as I hadn't wanted to bring any of Coral Wright's choices with me. I needed to choose a new name and create a very different person to the Bournemouth woman.

I felt the tension slowly leaving my body as the warm meal and wine began to take effect. I wouldn't rush back to the B & B, Liliad was comfortable and there was no TV in the room so it would be a long night. I guess it was being in an Italian restaurant again that took my mind back to Barry Mason. How reckless of him to think he could outwit me or think I would fold under his threat.

I felt more annoyance than remorse; the trouble he'd put me to when I'd done my best to avoid any confrontation; it was unforgiveable.

It was a bit concerning that he'd kept in touch with Lily's mother, Mrs Munroe and might have told her that he'd discovered me in Bournemouth but I doubted if anything they'd discussed ever got back to DCI Munroe knowing the long lasting tension that existed between him and Barry and remembering the frosty relationship I'd noticed in the past between Munroe and his wife I very much doubted that she would confide anything in him.

My thoughts led me on to DCI Munroe; it was odd he didn't seem to take centre stage in any of the TV interviews about my disappearance; that he directed questions to his sidekick, DI Wilson. It was unlike him to avoid the limelight. I wondered if he was ill, he certainly hadn't looked too good when he'd come to St Joseph's with news of my parents. I wondered how I could find out but did it matter? I sighed and sipped my wine, probably it didn't. I was well away now; there was no reason for anyone to think I'd be this far north. I put him out of my mind.

◆

Back in the room at the B & B Liliad seemed fine, totally absorbed watching people move about the town square below so I left her to it and squeezed myself into my minute en suite for a shower. At least the water was hot even if I did manage to bang my elbows on the shower walls as I washed my hair and nearly fell head first into the toilet as I stepped out. The sooner we could get to St Maabs the better.

Breakfast the next morning was surprisingly good; I found I was sharing the dining room with a business man, a family of three and a couple of elderly ladies who chatted animatedly with Mr Warren as he served up huge plates of traditional British fry up. Listening in on their conversation it appeared that, although quiet at the moment, the B & B was expecting an influx of guests the next weekend at the beginning of May, so I'd been correct in my belief that the holiday season was getting underway which would make my arrival in St Maabs less conspicuous.

Before I went out I placed Liliad back in the suitcase, 'In case they come in to service the room,' I explained. Recalling how chilled I'd felt the day before I donned a pullover under my tracksuit top. I didn't want to leave the rest of my money in the room so bundled it into my handbag. It was risky carrying it all but I didn't feel I had much choice. Firstly I'd replenish my clothes stock with more suitable attire and then call in on Brown and Wilson.

A couple of hours later I entered the letting agents clutching my several purchases and slumped onto a seat opposite a young woman who grinned at me from the opposite side of her desk. 'You look as though you've had a successful shop.'

'I have indeed but I'm knackered now.'

'How can I help you?'

I carefully laid my various bags on the floor. 'I wondered if you could give me some details about your cottages in St Maabs.'

'Are you looking for a holiday let or to rent long term?'

'I'd prefer to buy – is that possible?'

She hesitated, 'Maybe but they don't come up very often.'

'There was that one about six months ago but that was at St Maabs Head, not in the actual village.'

Surprised I turned in the direction of the voice to discover a man sitting in the shadows at the back of the office. He'd been so still and quiet I hadn't noticed him before.

'Oh yes, I'd forgotten that.' The woman went over to the filing cabinet. Talking with her back to me she continued, 'we were amazed that sold, it wasn't in a very good state and it's pretty near the edge.'

My puzzlement was obvious as she turned back toward me, an A4 sheet in her hand. 'The cliffs on the headland get a real battering in winter; there's been a lot of erosion over recent years.' She looked at the paper in her hand, 'Of course, all of that was reflected in the price and I suppose if you're not planning on staying there for years, it might be worth the gamble.'

'I don't think I'd want to gamble on it.' The man got up and walked toward us. He was about five foot seven, going slightly bald with a protruding belly but a cheerful countenance. He was surprisingly light and fluid in his movements; I reckoned he'd be a good dancer, probably ballroom. I held out my hand for the leaflet. 'May I take a look?'

The man introduced himself, 'Brian Reading,' and shook my hand before expanding on his earlier comments. 'It's really isolated up there on the Head, only four cottages remaining; all in poor condition and not properties that we're inclined to rent out. I recall the chap who bought that one, we tried to put him off but he was adamant; said he didn't want to live in the village. I think he was into this survival lark, you know, extreme living. Rather him than me.'

I looked at the sales leaflet. The photograph showed a granite two storey structure, a square block of a building, door in the centre with windows either side; two upstairs, two downstairs. Taken from some distance away, presumably to partially disguise the state of the place, the cottage appeared to be at the end of a narrow track that snaked up the headland through barren land, the sea below sheer cliffs on the one side and total desolation on the other. I couldn't imagine why anyone would want to live there.

My dismay obviously evident Brian rustled about in the filing cabinet and produced a brochure of their holiday lets in St Maabs itself. 'St Maabs is a very quaint village; got a general store, a pleasant pub and an afternoon tea room. It's very popular with the hiking, climbing and mountain biking fraternity. If you like, I can take you up there now and show you around some of our cottages; they vary quite a lot from basic to luxury depending on your requirements and your budget.'

'That's very good of you; it would be helpful. Maybe I could rent for a few weeks while I decide and wait to see if any sales do come up. Is there public transport from Berwick to St Maabs – I don't have a car.'

'Yes, a local bus runs four times a day so you wouldn't be stranded but I'll bring you back so you don't have to worry.'

I smiled with pleasure, 'Let's do that then.'

St Maabs was only about eight miles from Berwick along a mainly single track road that meandered through some of the most rugged, forbidding landscape I'd ever encountered and seemed to lead to St Maabs and nowhere else. Living here through the winter months was definitely not for the faint-hearted.

Brian chatted amiably all the way there filling me in on St Maabs history and what I could expect to find. 'It's a small village that tumbles down to a harbour. The cottages are old fishermen's homes but the place is now primarily a holiday destination. They offer deep sea angling, hiking trails, kayaking and mountain biking mainly. Then a little further up the coast is The Head, that's a popular place for bird enthusiasts. We get thousands of sea birds nesting on the sheer cliffs and you can get quite close … if you like that sort of thing. What's your interest?'

'Hiking and biking mainly.'

'So why do you want to *buy* here? Are you thinking of living here full time?'

'Maybe; I'm quite a loner so the solitary life appeals and it seems there's enough of a community here all year round. With Berwick so close total isolation, which I'd find too much, doesn't seem a problem.'

'That's true although there have been times in the winter when the road to Berwick has become impassable. Well, here we are.' He turned into a small car park. 'It's probably easier if we walk from here. We've got six cottages for rent all close together; three basic and three luxury so I'll take you in one of each if that's OK.'

From the car park we climbed steeply through the village passing the pub and general store on the way. 'As you can see, everything here is close together so not far to walk for anything,' he grinned, 'or stumble home from the pub of an evening.'

We turned down a side lane, Brian fumbling in his pocket for his keys. 'Right, this is a basic cottage.' One of a terraced row the cottage door was positioned to one side of the building and opened into a small entrance lobby. Immediately off to the left was a cosy lounge off which was a kitchen diner looking out the back to a small yard.

Stairs led up from the lounge to a double bedroom with bathroom off over the kitchen diner. 'As I said, a basic two up, two down but on your own plenty big enough I suppose.'

'It's nicely furnished,' I remarked, taking in the two seater sofa covered with a floral throw, the quite modern kitchen units and foldaway table and chairs and the log burning stove, 'but maybe a little too snug for me, especially if I decide on a long let.'

'Fair enough; the luxury cottages are basically twice the size and the fittings are a bit more upmarket. Let's look at one of those.'

Brian ushered me out of the door and we walked a little further up the lane until we came to a small green surrounded by detached cottages. These were more like the one in the photograph, the one at The Head that had been sold.

'These are more your family cottages.' Brian unlocked the door to a proper hallway with rooms off either side. To the left was a dining room leading through into the kitchen and on the right a large lounge. From the hall stairs rose up to a landing with two bedrooms and a bathroom. Once again, it was all cosily furnished but a more upmarket kitchen and a larger bathroom with bath and separate shower unit. Compared to what I was coping with at the B & B this was luxury indeed.

'I don't suppose you ever consider selling any of these?' I asked hopefully.

'No, afraid not but very occasionally a resident's cottage comes on the market. Apart from the people running the tourist activities the majority of permanent residents are quite elderly so they do come up sometimes. You just have to be patient and have time on your side.'

I thought for a moment, 'Your assistant said there were two or three other cottages up on The Head.'

'Mm, yeah but it's really wild up there and the coast is eroding at quite a rate, still it's entirely your decision. Have you ever been up there?'

I shook my head somewhat sheepishly. Brian gave a knowing smile, 'Well, may I suggest that you take a look before you go any further. As Katie said, there are a few cottages that are empty up there … which should speak for itself really … and they're cheaper. You need to have a look around, peer through the windows, see the general layout and the area. If after that you're still keen we'll help you locate the current owners.'

'That sounds like a good plan. OK, I'll take your advice and do that.'

We wandered back down through the village to the car. As we passed the pub I spotted a notice in the window asking for bar staff the really interesting part being that it said accommodation was included. I resolved to return the next day and enquire further.

Brian dropped me off outside the B & B; handing me my bags out of the car boot he said, 'I've tucked the cottage brochure into one of your bags; the prices and all the details are in there. Give me a call if you want to proceed with a rental or if there's anything else we can help you with.'

'Thank you, you've been most kind and helpful. I've got a lot to think over.' We shook hands and I bundled indoors and straight upstairs, eager to share the day's events with Liliad.

Sitting beside Liliad on the bed I outlined everything that had happened during the day and how I intended to proceed. She didn't seem particularly enthusiastic, her eyes frequently flitting to the side to look out of the window. I was a little peeved as I felt I'd really made some progress. 'What's the matter? I thought you'd be pleased that I'm moving things on.'

Her head turned fractionally in my direction and then toward the window again. It was now five thirty and the town square was busy with people shopping on their way home from work or enjoying a sociable coffee and chat at some of the cafes. 'Oh I see, you're afraid it'll all be too quiet in St Maabs. I guess it could be in the winter but not during the summer holiday season and if I manage to get the job at the pub there'll be loads going on … possibly music nights. If we develop a good relationship with the publican he might even let you stay behind the bar.'

Liliad looked a little doubtful at this final suggestion but allowed a brief nod to the possibility. I wrapped my arm around her, giving her a small hug of comfort. 'Let me show you the clothes I've bought and then, shall I get out the chess board? We've no TV so we might as well have a game before bed.'

By ten o'clock I called a halt to the game; I was so tired I could hardly keep my eyes open. Snuggling under the covers I left Liliad watching the night life in the town square as I tried to settle my thoughts. What if I was wrong and Philip Maccleson wasn't in St Maabs or, if he was but it turned out he wasn't my father either. The thought of failure coated my spirit like an opaque film. Knowing who I truly was and thereby gaining some insight into my psyche was unquestionably enticing but I'd also hoped all along that when I'd found my father I'd be able to manipulate him into supporting me in some way; after all, I hadn't cost him anything for thirty two years, it was about time he accepted some responsibility and I definitely didn't want to have to go back to full-time work. That didn't bear thinking about. After all this effort I deserved a positive, lucrative outcome.

Next morning I was one of the first down for breakfast as I wanted to get to the pub at St Maabs early to lessen the chance of someone beating me to the vacancy. As I didn't want to have to shut Liliad away in a cupboard I told Mr Warren there was no need to service my room. 'Service your room?' he exclaimed, 'What do you think this is, the bloody Hilton.' The sooner we could get out of here the better.

I dressed in some of the new clothes I'd bought; jeans, T-shirt, comfy trainers and a hooded jacket; the smart but casual look and headed for the bus stop. The day was cool but bright and clear, the bus on time with only three passengers including me. The countryside didn't seem quite so bleak in the sunshine and as the bus pulled in the view down to the harbour with the sea calm and sparkling, really lifted my spirits. There was so little traffic the overriding sounds were of screeching gulls and the gentle lap of the water.

Concerned that it was a bit early to go knocking on the pub door I wandered into the general store for a browse. The woman behind the counter was like everybody's favourite granny; round cheerful face, eyes that sparkled with mischief and a couple of chins that wobbled slightly as she spoke. I imagine any small child would love to be clasped to that ample bosom … not that I'd ever experienced any such thing.

'Anything I can help you with, dear?'

'No thanks, just having a browse.' I wandered down the aisle by the counter checking what was on the shelves.

'You staying here on holiday?'

It was obvious she wanted a chat and it occurred to me that she was probably a good source of information. 'Sort of,' I turned to face her, 'actually, I'd like to come for a long stay and maybe live here permanently if it works out. I see there's a vacancy for bar staff at the pub; I thought I'd make enquiries.'

She smiled warmly, 'You could do worse; Doug's a bit of a one off and takes some getting used to but he's got a heart of gold really, he just likes to keep it hidden.' She chuckled, 'They say round here that it's the only pub you go into to be insulted and that's about right. Some of the tourists find it a bit unsettling but the locals love it.'

'Thanks for the warning; I'll bear that in mind.'

'Have you done bar work before?'

I smiled ruefully, 'Only in my student days.'

'How's your mental arithmetic?'

'Not bad; why?'

'Just to warn you, Doug's still back in the dark ages as far as technology is concerned. It's all hand pumped beers and an old fashioned till; you'll have to learn the prices of all the drinks and add up in your head as you go along. Do you think you can do that?'

I grinned, 'With a bit of practice; I'm sure it'll come back to me.'

'Well you've got time to get used to it if you can start now; the holiday season isn't in full swing yet. It can get manic later in the year.'

'Thanks for the advice,' I glanced at my watch, 'better get over there.'

'Good luck; maybe see you around.'

'I hope so.' I hurried out the door. That little conversation had been very useful; at least now I had some idea of what to expect.

The sun had increased in strength while I'd been in the store causing me to remove my jacket and sling it over my arm as I strolled toward the pub. A salty tang permeated the air tickling my nostrils and feeling like a mild antiseptic cleansing my airways and my spirit, creating an optimism I fervently prayed wasn't misplaced.

I rapped my knuckles on the front door of the pub; I could hear barrels being rolled and scraped over the ground in the back yard so I waited a few minutes but having received no response walked around to the back.

A large man, not fat but solidly built and over six feet tall had his back to me as he stacked beer barrels against the far wall. Shirt sleeves rolled up to his elbows exposing muscular brown arms covered with a light down of hair, loose fitting trousers held by a leather belt positioned below the trouser waist band; he looked like a character out of a Dickens novel.

'Hello.' Receiving no reply I tried again, 'Excuse me.'

He turned, one hand still resting on the barrel he'd been about to lift. 'Why, what have you done?'

Confused by his response I stammered, 'Er, nothing.'

'Well, if you just want to be excused you are, so off you go,' and he turned back to his work.

I stood there, mouth agape, trying to decide how to proceed. I now understood the store woman's observations. 'I see you're advertising for bar staff.'

Keeping his back to me he said, 'I know that already.'

OK, two can play at this game. I smiled sweetly, 'I'm sure you do but what you don't know is that I'd like to apply.'

'I think I could have figured that out. Done bar work before have you?' He turned to face me his hands clasped to his back as he stretched up to his full height, easing the creaks in his spine.

'Yes I have.'

'Students Union bar was it; a glass of Pimms and a bag of cashews,' he snorted derisively.

'Actually it was more two pints of lager and a packet of crisps.'

He allowed himself a slight grin as his eyes travelled over me. 'Not much of you is there,' he observed, 'you'll be no bloody use down in the cellar when it comes to changing barrels.'

'No, but I've got you to do that while I charm the customers.'

His grin widened. 'Come inside and we'll talk a bit more.'

I followed him into the back entrance; a short corridor that led off to ladies and gents toilets either side and straight in front to the bar lounge area. Doug had to duck his head to get through the doorway and at places in the bar where the beams lowered the ceiling height yet he moved with a smoothness and lack of hesitation that spoke of years of practise, his every movement about the place instinctive.

He indicated a table in the corner flanked by a couple of high backed wooden benches, winged at head height making it a cosy little noke. Squeezing in opposite me he laid his arms on the table, leaning slightly forward. 'What brings you here?'

'The notice for the job vacancy.'

He sighed. 'No, I mean what brings you to an out of the way place like St Maabs? Are you running away from something?'

'What? No!' His question shook me slightly, coming as it did so near the truth. 'I'm a respectable woman, thank you very much.'

He leant back on the bench, no sign of embarrassment at his pointed questioning. 'So, I ask again, what brings you here?'

I decided on the most commonplace and plausible. 'I've recently been made redundant from a high powered job in London and it's given me space to think. I want to try a more relaxed pace of living but I need to be sure it's truly what I want before I purchase a place to live. I thought this job, with the accommodation on offer was a good place to start and it'll help me get to know people and what it's like living and working somewhere like this. I can't afford to just retire, I'm only thirty two.' I paused, 'It isn't that unusual.'

He nodded in agreement, 'You're right, it isn't. OK, let me show you the accommodation ... you might change your mind. Oh, by the way, are you OK with dogs?'

'Yes, I love them.'

'Just as well, I've got three.' He stood and I followed him through the pub, down a couple of steps in the main bar and through a door marked 'Private.' Stairs ran steeply up to another floor. 'My flat is on this level.' He waved a hand to indicate the length of the corridor with various doors off, 'and up here is your bedsit, if you want the job that is.' Directly ahead some more stairs led into an airy roof space lit by a couple of dormer windows and a couple of skylights. A very large room that ran the length of the pub it was adequately furnished and although open plan divided quite cleverly into kitchen area, sitting area and bedroom. Behind a door at the far end was a shower room and toilet.

The smell of polish and pine disinfectant combined with the morning sun that illuminated the whole room gave a feeling of spaciousness that the slanted ceiling did nothing to detract. Coupled with views out over the harbour and the vast expanse of sea I fell in love with it instantly and I just knew Liliad would adore it.

'It's lovely,' I said beaming from ear to ear, 'when can I start?'

'Tell you what if you want to move in this weekend you can start work on Monday. It's always the quietest day so it'll give me time to show you the ropes and for you to familiarise yourself with where everything is. I'm happy to pay you cash in hand provided you're only working for me during the summer season; if you stay on any longer it'll have to be on a more formal footing.'

'That suits me fine, I'll see you Saturday, say about eleven.'

We shook hands; mine lost in the firm grip of his gorilla sized palm. Just as I was leaving he called, 'I forgot to ask; what's your name?'

'Veronica Maddox but everyone calls me Vee.'

He raised a hand in acknowledgement. I fairly skipped back up through the village to the bus stop. Being paid as casual labour was ideal; it meant I didn't have to worry about documentation for my new identity. I hoped that by the end of the summer I'd have found my father and could adopt my *true* identity at last.

CHAPTER 21

I bounded up the stairs of the B & B bursting in upon Liliad who was in her usual place on the bed, gazing out to the Square below. 'I got it, the job at the pub and we can move in over the weekend. The accommodation is great, you'll love it; fantastic views out over the harbour to the sea – a much better view than the flat in Bournemouth.' I paused for breath, dropping onto the bed beside her.

Disappointed at her lack of enthusiasm I forcibly turned her to face me. Her eyes, usually so wide and unflinching seemed to narrow; her caution or was it outright distrust glinting from their oriental looking slits. 'What's the matter? Don't you want me to find my real father?'

As we stared at each other something gnawed at my gut that wasn't hunger. Liliad's apprehension was making me nervous; perhaps there was a risk involved, Liliad obviously thought there was, that it would be best left alone but I just couldn't. Why couldn't she understand that? 'Please, Liliad don't make me doubt.'

Her expression softened slightly as she leant a little closer toward me, a tiny olive branch of acceptance. I grasped it eagerly, hugging her close. 'It'll be alright, I promise.'

I knew this was another of my long shots but what else did I have. I was sick of people making my life difficult, it was bad enough always being alone without the likes of Alberto, Barry Mason and bloody Munroe causing me problems. If only I could find my father. I felt that somehow it would ground me; give me an understanding of what made me tick not to mention the fact that I was getting to the point where some financial help wouldn't go amiss. Even if he didn't offer to contribute to my well-being voluntarily it was likely that a unacknowledged daughter turning up on his doorstep could be an inducement to open his wallet. The possibilities in that respect were several.

Liliad held my gaze for a few pregnant moments, then allowed her eyelids to slowly lower as she turned toward the window once more and I sensed sadness in her I couldn't understand. I had to get her completely on side; somehow persuade her.

'I've taken the job at the pub because the accommodation's free and it's the best way to get to know the locals; make connections that might help my enquiries but I've also looked at cottages to buy or rent because I know we need to put down roots. I promise that even if my father isn't in St Maabs, even if I've got everything completely wrong, I will stop looking and settle. I really believe we'll both love living there. It's a really pretty village, busy in the summer but not dead during the winter months and I like Berwick too so we can have the best of both worlds and it's a long way away from Inspector Munroe and St Joseph's. So you see, I have thought this through.'

Liliad's only response was an almost imperceptible nod of her head.

Saturday morning I stuffed myself with breakfast, determined to get my money's worth out of the miserable Mr Warren. Then, dragging my suitcase with Liliad once again nestled inside I left without saying a word; I didn't want any awkward questions. I'd paid up to the Monday and was sure that provided he'd got his money Mr Warren wouldn't give a damn whether I was there or not.

The bus to St Maabs was once again on time and I settled into my seat to enjoy the journey. It was a shame that

Liliad couldn't share it with me but then, maybe when she saw our new accommodation and that wonderful view over the harbour she would forgive all the inconveniences I'd put her through.

As the bus crested the rise the little village spread out before us, its cottages meandering down to the harbour where holiday sailing craft bobbed alongside a few commercial fishing vessels, riding the swell like horses straining for the 'off'.

The St Maabs Head pub was situated about halfway down to the harbour, the slope so steep I had to hang on tightly to my wheeled suitcase to stop it running away from me. The last thing Liliad needed was a dunking in the water; she'd *never* be on side if that happened.

The pub door swung open at my knock, stepping over the threshold I called, 'Mr Doug ...' and realised I didn't know his last name. 'Anyone there? Doug, its Veronica Maddox, Vee, the new barmaid.'

Suddenly the place erupted with the sound of barking, yelping and the frantic scratch and scraping of a multitude of claws on wooden stairs before the door behind the bar burst open and three mutts of varying sizes and shapes hurtled toward me. Instinctively I hoisted my suitcase up before me as protection as I backed toward the door which had swung shut behind me. A huge, shaggy tornado of hair and flesh skidded to a halt on the boarded floor, sliding toward me on its belly as a black and white Terrier used it as a springboard to leap at me, almost at head height closely followed by a rather sedate Afghan Hound that held slightly back, eyeing me with disdain.

'I thought you said you liked dogs.'

Doug shuffled toward me running his fingers through an unruly mop of hair looking as though he'd just got up.

'I do but not all at once.'

'Rufus, get down!' Doug's bark was almost as loud as the dogs. 'They won't hurt you, just lick you to death.' The Terrier stopped acting like a springbok and sat. The tornado, a Retriever stood, trying to stick its muzzle into my pocket.

'Bruno's expecting a treat.' Doug explained.

'Well, I'm afraid he's going to be disappointed unless he'd like a fluff covered mint.'

Doug grinned, 'Welcome; c'mon I'll help you upstairs with your case.' He lifted my suitcase with the ease of a man used to hefting heavy objects and led the way upstairs. Pushing open the door to my flat he dropped the case just inside. 'I'll leave you to sort yourself out. The village shop is open until six tonight so I suggest you get yourself stocked up with a few necessities and this evening come down to the pub and make yourself acquainted with a few of the customers. It's mainly the village regulars but there'll soon be a lot more faces once the holiday makers arrive so it'll be easier for you if you get to know a few locals first – make you feel more at home. Up to you of course.'

'Yes I will; thanks. It's a good idea.'

'Right, I'll leave you to it,' and he was gone.

Unzipping the suitcase I carefully lifted Liliad out, holding her close I turned her to face the window for the view down across the harbour and out to the horizon. 'You see, I told you it was magnificent.' I could feel the pleasure ripple between us and I just knew everything would be alright. Lifting her strings I walked her carefully across the floor and up onto the sofa back before placing her in the sunshine on the deep windowsill. She settled immediately her gaze transfixed on the activities below.

I bustled around unpacking our few things. There was a coffee table before the sofa on which I placed the chess board and pieces. 'There, it feels like home already.' I checked out the bathroom and kitchen cupboards. There were a few items but it seemed that I needed quite a lot to get us through the next couple of days. 'If you're OK I'm going to pop down to the general store and get us stocked up.' Liliad nodded without taking her eyes off the view. I grinned to myself as I picked up my handbag, refraining from saying 'I told you so.'

The general store was at the top of the steep hill. As I climbed I was painfully aware of how unfit I was, my legs protesting and my breath coming in short, ragged gasps as I neared the top. There being little to do here other than physical activities I realised I had no excuse. I was thirty two years old, fast approaching middle age; I needed to take myself in hand if I was to truly enjoy the benefits of living here.

'Well hello, dear; you've come back; did you get the job at the pub?' It was the same woman behind the shop counter as before.

'Yes I did, thank you and thanks again for your advice, I'm sure it helped.'

'No problem; It's always better to be forewarned about our Dougie. What can I help you with?'

'If you don't mind I think I'll just wander around and decide as I see things, the cupboards are quite bare at the moment.' I picked up a wire basket and started down the first aisle.

'Of course, just let me know if you need any help.' So saying she picked up a bundle of magazines and turning toward the rack began re-arranging the display.

I wandered down the aisles, picking up essential every-day items along with a few culinary treats. The shop was surprisingly well-stocked and must do a lucrative trade during the holiday season.

Heaving the basket up onto the counter so that my items could be checked through the till I volunteered, 'My name's Vee by the way.'

'Margaret,' she offered, not breaking stride as she scanned my purchases. Handing back my shopping, now carefully packed into two carrier bags she said, 'Good luck with the job, no doubt you'll be serving *me* before the weeks' out!'

'I look forward to it.' I placed a bag in each hand for balance as I negotiated the exit into the street, the weight of my shopping seeming to propel me down the hill at an alarming rate; I really did need to up my fitness levels.

By the time I'd climbed the two flights of stairs into the apartment I was exhausted. Dropping the shopping on the floor just inside the door I slumped onto the sofa, feeling as though my arms had been pulled out of their sockets. Thank goodness Doug wasn't expecting me to work tonight – I didn't think I'd be able to stand much less pull a pint.

The day passed in a haze of contentment; I organised cupboards, moved some of the furniture to suit my taste, gave the bathroom and kitchen a quick once over with the cleaning materials I'd bought – it wasn't bad but I felt better when it gleamed and smelt cared for. By six in the evening everything was to my satisfaction; I sat down to one of the ready meals I'd bought gazing out toward the harbour as the sun sank slowly, painting a red hue onto the surface of the water like spilled wine. It was so picturesque I could have sat all evening until the light completely failed but remembering Doug's suggestion that I spend some time in the pub getting to know people I had a quick shower and change and, a little nervously, made my way down the stairs.

CHAPTER 22

Entering the bar a sudden draught snatched the stair door out of my hand, shutting it with a resounding bang. Eight pairs of eyes turned in my direction as two tables of four elderly men stopped in mid-motion and stared with ill-disguised hostility. I gave a thin, apologetic smile and whispered, 'Sorry,' as they all turned their attention back to the job in hand, namely playing dominoes.

As I slid out from behind the bar and walked through to the lounge area my heels, to compound my embarrassment, clacked on the wooden floor; the only sound other than the click of dominoes on table surfaces. Doug, behind the bar, gave me a wicked grin. 'Take a seat, Vee. What can I get you?'

'I think I'll have a large G and T please.' I looked around the room. 'Quiet in here isn't it?'

'It's early yet; regulars tend to have their regular times. By nine you won't recognise the place. It's my fault, I should have told you to wait until later; I'd forgotten it was the last night of the local dominoes tournament – it's a serious business.'

'So it would seem.' I took a large swig of G and T. 'Will they ever forgive me?'

'Yeah, they're a friendly crowd – once the game's over. Is everything OK in the flat?'

'Perfect; thank you.'

Suddenly the other room erupted with the sound of hands being banged on tables. 'That's it,' Doug commented, 'now the serious drinking will begin. Come down to the lower bar with me, I know what they all want to drink so you can give them waitress service for once and say your hello. Gents, this is Vee, our new barmaid.' Doug waved a hand in my direction.

'Thank God for that, a pretty face behind the bar instead of having to look at your ugly mug all night.' This was greeted with loud guffaws and 'Here, here'. The speaker held out his hand to me. 'Nice to meet you, Vee; I'm Geoff and these reprobates are Jim, Andy and Reg. Why don't you join us for a few minutes and tell us a bit about yourself.'

I glanced across at the bar where Doug had placed another four drinks for the second table. 'There's really not much to tell and it looks as though I've some more waitressing to do, but thanks anyway,' and I swiftly moved away before he could insist.

Doug was right, they were a friendly crowd; if I'd accepted all the drinks I was offered during the evening I'd have been seriously drunk.

As Doug had said by nine o'clock the place was buzzing. OK, it was a Saturday night but if this was what Doug termed "quiet", I could imagine what the holiday season must be like.

By the end of the evening I'd made the acquaintance of so many people my head was spinning. I'd exchanged a few passing pleasantries, finding out more about the area and its locals whilst managing to divulge very little about my own circumstances. As to why I'd come to St Maabs I gave the same answer I'd given Doug; I wanted a less stressful life and change had been forced upon me due to redundancy. It was an explanation that seemed to satisfy most people.

During the evening I kept my ears alert but the only 'Phil' I heard mentioned turned out to be a man in his eighties sitting in a corner nursing a pint of Guinness and the local newspaper.

Despite my eagerness to move things on I stopped myself asking too many questions; there was no point arousing suspicion; I'd take things slowly. Once I was behind the bar it would be easy to raise the occasional question as I worked – it would seem like the usual innocuous chitchat people expect with their bar staff.

Dragging myself up the two flights of stairs to the flat I was overcome with fatigue; the stress of the past couple of weeks combined with my investigations and move had taken their toll. Hardly bothering to properly clean my teeth much less remove my makeup I collapsed into bed and didn't wake until nine thirty the next morning. I couldn't recall the last time I'd had such a deep, satisfying sleep. However my search for my biological father turned out I was beginning to feel that coming to St Maabs was the best move I'd ever made.

Sitting beside Liliad on the deep windowsill I ate a leisurely breakfast of toast and coffee as in contemplative silence we both gazed out to sea. There was a light breeze that plucked at the rigging of the pleasure yachts in the harbour, setting up a musical harp-like tinkling. The sun, warming us both through the window glass, illuminated the still surface of the water creating slightly distorted reflections of the various craft.

As the minutes passed the numbers of people slowly increased until the whole area was a buzz of activity.

Unexpectedly I felt a sudden urge to be part of it all. 'I'm going for a walk,' I announced to Liliad as I slid down from the windowsill and headed to the bedroom for my outdoor clothes.

As I neared the harbour the scent of fishy saltiness increased until it left a tang in my mouth as though I'd had kippers for breakfast rather than a couple of pieces of toast. I leant on the harbour wall, watching the seagulls circling and screeching overhead then directed my gaze down to the men on the quay. Geoff, one of the domino players, was sitting mending fishing nets. I strolled down to him. 'Hello, Geoff.'

He looked up at the sound of my voice, his hands in suspension above his work. 'Hello, Vee.'

'You look as though you've done that before.' I indicated the net.

'Just once or twice.'

'May I watch?'

'Sure, you can have a go if you like.'

I grinned ruefully, 'I don't think you'll want me to do that. I constantly drop stitches when I knit and in any case I think there's more of a skill to that than you're implying.'

His smile was lovely, his eyes crinkling at their corners; deep blue in a bronzed and weather-worn face. I reckoned he was in his early fifties, about the same age I thought Philip Maccleson would be.

'Have you lived here long?'

'All my life,' he said, bending his head once more to his work.

'Do you mind all the tourists?'

He sighed quietly, 'It's hard to mind when they bring in so much money and a small community like this needs the income, there's not much else here that generates money. Not much for the youngsters.'

'But you get some new residents, don't you? A few who want to make St Maabs their permanent home?'

'A few.' He raised his head to look directly at me, 'Usually people running away from something.'

His comment echoed Doug's question at my interview. I met his gaze, 'Or maybe running *toward* something; something more positive and reaffirming in their lives.'

'Mm, maybe; guess I'll never know, will I?'

We eyed one another, an unspoken understanding between us. I turned my head and gazed out to sea; a boat was on its way into harbour; I could just make out two men on board.

Geoff noticed my interest. 'That'll be Stan back from taking someone deep sea angling.'

'I wonder if they've caught anything.' I watched as the skipper expertly guided the small boat to dock. His passenger gathered up his fishing gear and shook hands before disembarking and walking along the quay past where

Geoff and I were sitting. He was of medium height and build with a thatch of black hair and deep set, wide eyes.

'Catch anything?' I asked as he drew level.

He hardly broke stride as he turned his head toward me, his look cold and penetrating. 'May have,' he said as he continued walking.

I stared at his retreating back, feeling embarrassment colour my face. 'That was friendly,' I remarked to Geoff.

Geoff kept his eyes focussed on mending his net. 'Bit of a loner, that one.' It was plain from his demeanour that the subject was closed. I stood, brushing down the seat of my jeans. 'I think I'll explore a bit more. See you in the pub sometime I expect.'

'Indeed you will, my lovely. Bye.'

I turned and climbed the steps back up to the main street, deciding to take an idle wander around the village back streets and maybe pop into the café for lunch. I wasn't yet sure just when the bulk of my hours in the pub would be. Doug and I had agreed to see how busy things became and adjust accordingly. That suited me fine; I intended to be as co-operative as I could manage as creating a good impression was important if I did decide to put down roots.

CHAPTER 23

By mid-June St Maabs was pulsing with energy, tourists multiplying by the day; the place was awash with mountain bikes, paddle boards, fishing and hiking gear and working in the St Maabs Head my feet barely touched the ground. I had Mondays off as it was always a little quieter then but otherwise found myself working a hectic six day week. Doug kept the cellar functioning while I was responsible for stocking up behind the bar. There was a kitchen out the back staffed by a husband and wife team who provided the usual pub fare – nothing spectacular but it seemed to go down well with the tourists and locals alike. A Mrs Brownlow came in each morning to clean for which I was eternally grateful; at my interview

I'd forgotten to ask and had been afraid that would be down to me as well.

Despite having once taught in college I'd never been on my feet for so long before and found the first couple of weeks agonising but eventually my body got used to all the standing. Doug did provide me with a stool behind the bar but I seldom got much time to sit on it. Each night I fell exhausted into my bed and slept the sleep of the dead until the screech of seagulls and harbour noises would wake me early next morning.

A real plus was that my mental arithmetic improved astronomically and within a few weeks I found I not only knew the cost of drinks and mixers by heart but was adding up large varied orders in my head and still managing to have a sociable chat with the customers.

The tourist visitors were little more than a blur of faces all merging into one nondescript mass but I found I was beginning to recognise and easily pick out the locals. I'd become quite friendly with Geoff and his dominoes crowd and Margaret from the general store and her husband but as for having the opportunity to glean information that might help in my search for my father I was simply too busy. I realised that I'd either have to wait until things quietened down in the winter months or perhaps chat in the general and hardware stores and café on my Mondays off.

As frustrating as the delay was I was feeling more and more that I wanted St Maabs to be my permanent home regardless of the outcome of my search.

By the end of June I'd been living and working in St Maabs for six weeks. I hadn't formed any friendships that had resulted in one to one socialising but that didn't bother me; I was used to life being just Liliad and myself and found the arms-length socialising in the pub and shops quite to my liking; that way there was no chance of my being asked awkward questions.

Liliad seemed blissfully happy perched on her windowsill looking out over the harbour; in fact she was so contented we hadn't even bothered to start a game of chess, instead the set merely sat on the coffee table gathering dust. I too felt little desire to upset the status quo until, that is, one Sunday evening.

It was almost closing time, the bar had thinned out considerably when the entrance door opened and the man I'd spoken to so briefly on the quay walked in. Striding purposefully toward the bar, looking neither right nor left, he slammed some coins down and loudly said, 'A glass of Bull's Blood.' His voice was deep and gravelly, the words coarse as if rubbed over the surface of a rasp.

I stared him out. '*Please*'. I placed my hands on the bar surface close to the flung coins but didn't pick them up. His gaze locked with mine, the silence between us growing louder with unspoken menace but I wasn't going to back down. Suddenly I became aware of Doug at my elbow.

'I'll get that,' he said as he scooped up the loose change. 'Why don't you collect up those glasses, Vee.' He indicated two tables just vacated near the door.

I shot him a look of annoyance but said nothing; as I walked from behind the bar I heard him say, 'Drink up, you've only got ten minutes before I close.'

The man downed his drink in one draught, slammed the glass onto the bar and, without even glancing in my direction, walked out into the night.

'You didn't have to do that,' I said to Doug, petulance sharpening my tone, ' I could have handled him.'

'Maybe you could but it's best not.' Doug responded; with a shrug he continued, 'It's been a long week, I'll finish off down here, you go and get your beauty sleep.'

'Ok, if you're sure.' I stacked the dirty glasses on the bar and hauled myself upstairs to the flat.

Liliad was watching the harbour lights as the moon cast a whitish sheen over the water. I settled down beside her, running my hand over her glossy black hair. 'I think tomorrow I'll have a chat with Margaret in the general store, I'm sure she's a mine of information and then I'll go up to The Head, have a look around.'

She turned her head slightly observing me from the corner of her eyes. 'I want to see those other cottages the agent said were up there,' I said by way of explanation, 'they're apparently not in good condition so they'll be cheaper to buy and if we want to stay here we need a proper place of our own; I don't want to be tied to this job for ever just because of the flat.'

The reason I'd given Liliad wasn't the whole truth. The stranger fascinated me; the way people seemed to say so little about him added to the mystery. I'd never seen him in any of the village shops and Sunday night was the first time he'd come into the pub.

I didn't have a clue who he was but I was intrigued not least because of the obvious dislike of the locals. I wanted to find out more.

◆

Monday morning arrived shrouded in a thick sea mist that rubbed its back around the buildings with sinuous feline grace. The silence was palpable; even the seagulls were quiet and the tinkling rigging of the yachts stilled as though a huge hand held them fast.

As I made my way up the hill in the direction of The Head it was as though I was totally alone in a surreal world of indistinguishable shapes.

I hoped the mist would thin as I climbed but it hung like a damask curtain blocking the view. Maybe this wasn't such a good idea in the circumstances but I didn't want to turn back and told myself it would clear as soon as a breeze got up. Anyway, if I was thinking of living up on The Head no doubt I'd have to get used to worse weather than this, especially during the winter months.

Fortunately the path to the top was a well-trodden track wide enough for a vehicle so as long as I stayed within its edges I couldn't go wrong. I knew it was a safe distance from the cliff edge and at least the mist would deter the hordes of bird watchers.

I kept my eyes downcast, concentrating on where I was placing my feet. The last few metres were particularly steep and a couple of times I wrung my ankle on the loose stones as I made the final ascent. Stopping for breath I straightened up, hands on hips and peered, attempting to penetrate the wet shroud that swirled around me. At least the breeze had picked up creating windows of clarity within the opaque wall suddenly bringing one of the cottages into view.

I felt a rush of achievement and quickened my pace, ridiculously afraid that the window would close and I would lose the vision for ever. I needn't have worried; the air was definitely shifting dispelling the mist little by little as a watery shaft of light from a determined sun cut through the gauze.

The agents hadn't been exaggerating when they'd said these cottages were in a sorry state of repair. As the mist cleared still further it disclosed three dwellings about four metres apart, all built with their backs to the sea, standing in a neat row like soldiers on parade and a fourth, standing alone precariously close to the cliff edge.

I went to each cottage in turn rubbing my sleeve on the windows to peer inside. It wasn't very inspiring, the layout of each was identical; presumably the landowner felt his workers just needed housing like so much cattle.

There were no windows in the rear walls so the single cottage by the cliff edge, built to an identical pattern, looked onto nothing but blank back walls – it was the most depressing sight.

Despite the rotten wooden windows and doors the granite construction was still sturdy so they could be salvaged but realistically that wasn't going to happen, especially by me. Heating was obviously by open fires, there was no electricity so you'd need your own generator and the only fresh water supply seemed to be a stream I'd passed on the way up.

Yet the agents had said the one standing alone had been sold. I wandered across to take a look just as the sun finally broke through the last of the mist. The view from up here was so spectacular it took my breath away as I stood, mesmerised by the expanse of sea and the hundreds of sea birds whirling about their nests in the cliff face, sending a cacophony of noise heavenward. Forcing my attention back to the cottage I carefully looked about me; there was no sign of anyone about so I approached cautiously, picking my way over the slabs laid out as a stepping stone path to the front door.

Moving to one side I looked through a downstairs window into a kitchen that ran the depth of the building. There was a sink with single drainer, a few floor and wall cupboards and a small formica topped table on which the remnants of someone's breakfast still lay.

I moved across to the other side of the front door. This was a sitting room; an open fire held dead ashes although there was a stack of logs to one side, a small two shelf bookcase crammed with paperbacks and another table close to the window with two chairs. By the fire was a deep seated armchair that had seen better days and everything was covered with a thick layer of dust. There was nothing cosy or welcoming about the place and if it hadn't been for the breakfast things I would have concluded that it hadn't been lived in for some time.

I stepped back to look up at the first floor windows wondering whether both rooms were bedrooms or if an internal bathroom had been created. As I stared I thought I saw a slight movement but dismissed it as the reflection of a bird overhead. I put my hand up to my forehead to shield my eyes from the brightness of the sun when a hand suddenly rapped the window pane like the crack of a pistol. Shocked I stumbled backwards, almost falling as I tripped over one of the path stepping stones.

Panicked I ran like a guilty child ducking behind the other cottages out of sight. Breathing hard I stood listening, waiting for someone to burst out of the front door after me. With relief I heard the chatter of a group of birdwatchers as they made their way up the track. I waited until they got a little closer then walked down toward them. 'You've been out early,' one of them remarked as we passed.

'Well you know what they say about the early bird..' I joked as I hurried back toward the village, stumbling slightly as I negotiated the steep downward slope.

Popping into the general store I grabbed a bottle of still water opening it immediately and taking a swig. Holding it up toward Margaret for inspection I said, 'Sorry, I will pay for this; I'm just *so* thirsty.'

'You look worn out; wherever have you been?'

'Up on The Head; I was intrigued by those old cottages up there and wanted to have a look around. Does anyone live up there? It seems awfully grim.'

Margaret leant forward onto the counter top as though settling in for a long chat. 'They've been empty for years, ever since the heart went out of the fishing industry. They're still owned by the local laird, he's been trying to sell them for ages but no-one's interested. To get electricity or running water to them would cost a fortune – in fact I doubt it's possible – so even the tourists aren't interested. Not many people like to rough it anymore; too used to mod cons.'

I wandered over to the counter, picking up a local newspaper on the way. 'Oh, I'm surprised; when I was talking to one of the letting agents about holiday lets here they did mention that one of them had been sold so I assumed they were a viable proposition.'

Margaret's face seemed to set slightly as she pushed herself up from the counter. 'Yes, you're right one was sold about a year ago. No-one could believe it; the man must have a death wish!'

'Why do you say that?'

'Because the cliff's being undermined by the sea; each winter more of the cliff face is lost, it's only a matter of time. When the locals discovered what he was planning several tried to dissuade him but he wouldn't listen – or else he just didn't care. Ever since he's kept to himself up there; not that anyone here in the village made him particularly welcome; folk don't like their best advice being ignored – smacks of arrogance.'

I nodded in agreement. 'There was a chap came in the pub last night. I hadn't seen him before, I wonder if that was him – medium height, had really black hair, in his fifties I'd say.'

'Sounds like him.'

'I wonder what he does all day,' I mused, 'stuck up there on his own.'

'Don't know, don't want to know. All I do know is that he comes down into the village about once a month, buys his groceries and a load of booze and when the weather's OK he goes out on the boat with Stan deep sea angling but that's about it. My advice is stay well away; he's a strange one.'

'Oh, I will.' I handed over the half-drunk bottle of water and newspaper for scanning. 'See you in the pub Friday?'

'We'll be there,' Margaret responded, 'regular as clockwork.'

I stepped out into the street turning all Margaret had told me over in my head. I was still curious about the man. Maybe I'd chat with Stan; he might know a bit more if they spent hours together on the boat. I didn't want to ask Margaret any more in case she started wondering too much about *me* and why I was so interested.

CHAPTER 24

The weeks sped by and it was the middle of August before I got a chance to have a word with Stan. Liliad and I had spent hours watching the activity down on the quay; the good weather encouraging day trippers as well as the long-term holiday makers. Stan's boat seemed to hardly be back in harbour before it was out again but one Monday I caught up with him early in the evening as he was tidying up.

'Hello, Stan, you've been busy lately.'

'Hi, Vee, yes I have; got to make hay as they say. How are you finding life in St Maabs?'

'I'm loving it.'

'And working for our Doug, how are you finding that?'

I grinned a little ruefully, 'He's fine, a bit eccentric but I like that – makes it fun.' I shuffled from one foot to the other as though embarrassment was making me hesitant. 'I've never been on a boat.'

'What! Well we can't have that, can we? How about I take you out next Monday evening when you're off work. Give you a trip along the coast.'

'That would be fantastic – thanks.'

I was thrilled. It was true that I hadn't been on a boat except once I'd done a short river cruise; hardly the same thing and it would give me a chance to quiz Stan about his mysterious passenger.

I told Liliad about it later that evening but she didn't seem too pleased. I was puzzled. 'It's quite safe, I'm sure; Stan's been working this coastline for years.'

Liliad seemed to shift slightly on the windowsill, her head inclining toward the chess set gathering dust on the coffee table.

'You want a game of chess? OK.' I took hold of her strings and lifted her down, walking her across to the sofa. Positioning her so she could reach I got a cushion and placed it on the other side on the floor and sat down myself. Taking a pawn in each hand I held them out to her. 'Choose,' I said. Her eyes indicated my left hand. I opened my fingers. 'You're white,' I said and twisted the board round. 'You start.'

We'd both made our opening and follow up moves when I mentioned the stranger. 'I'll be able to ask Stan a bit about him when I'm on the boat.'

Suddenly Liliad toppled forward off the sofa, her head crashing down onto the coffee table knocking over several of the chess pieces. I shot up, quickly raising her back and gently rubbing her forehead. 'I'm sorry, I couldn't have positioned you properly.'

Her eyes widened, the green of the irises catching the sun and flashing like warning beacons at me before she turned her head once more to the chess board. 'So that's what's worrying you; my interest in our enigmatic stranger. Well, there's no need, I know how to play the game or do you think I need a refresher course in tactics and strategy? Well, perhaps you're right, I need to focus and chess is the ideal way to enhance my concentration. I promise I'll be careful.'

Liliad kept looking at the chess board. Obediently I repositioned the displaced pieces. 'Let's start again,' I said.

◆

Liliad didn't want to go back on the windowsill but insisted on us playing chess every day for the following week. A couple of times I tried to resist but her hostile stare made me acquiesce. It was as though she was indicating it really was for my own good however irksome it felt. Nonetheless I was quite relieved when Monday evening came around and I could make my escape onto Stan's boat.

He took hold of my hand to help me on board. 'I've really been looking forward to this, Stan; thanks so much.'

'My pleasure, m'dear; we'll go northwards, that's the most spectacular and will give you a view of the seabirds nesting in the cliff face. You get a completely different perspective from the sea.'

I settled down on one of the benches, breathing in the scent of salt and fish. The wind was light so I wasn't worried I'd disgrace myself by being sick although I did find even the slight rolling motion made it difficult to keep my balance.

'You'll get the hang of it,' Stan encouraged me and he was right; by the time we made land again I was walking about the boat like a pro.

Viewed from the boat the sheer scale of the cliff face was awesome and as we came toward The Head the erosion was plain to see, reaching up toward the summit. 'I didn't realise the erosion was so extensive,' I remarked, 'or that the sea can be so destructive.'

'Aye, the sea's a powerful beast not to be dismissed lightly. In winter the swell here can be terrible; combine a high tide with storm conditions and you've a ferocious battering ram that can go on for days. No coast can withstand that, year in, year out.'

I looked up, shielding my eyes with my hand. I could see the cottage standing alone; defiant yet vulnerable. I pointed. 'Does anyone live up there?'

'Yes, but I should think not for much longer.'

'But why would anyone want to?'

'Some people believe the rules don't apply to them, that they can challenge nature and come out on top.' Stan paused as though considering. 'He'll learn.'

I turned on the bench to face him. 'Who's he?'

'Philip Maccleson.'

The name slammed into me like a gauntleted fist, my mouth agape with surprise. Stan noticed my shock. 'You know him?'

I gathered my wits. 'No, not at all. Who is he?'

'Don't rightly know. He moved here about a year ago, bought that place and moved in; since then kept himself much to himself. Comes out with me deep sea angling twice a week but that's about it. Secretive sort of bloke. Plenty of rumours about him as you might imagine.'

'What kind of rumours?'

Stan shrugged and turned looking out to sea. 'Words are water – one drop of rumour could drown you; that's why I don't repeat anything I hear. He's no trouble to anyone so best leave him alone is my opinion.'

I slumped into myself, my mind struggling to make sense of what Stan had said. If that surly brute was Philip Maccleson then Philip Maccleson couldn't possibly be my father; my mother would *never* have a relationship with a man like that, it was inconceivable. I felt my spirits plummet, all the energy drained out of me. It seemed that my search was a complete waste of time, as elusive and pointless as searching for the Holy Grail; my father wasn't in St Maabs, he couldn't be; there was no-one else even remotely likely. Despite my earlier assertions that it didn't matter one way or the other I now realised that it *did* matter; it mattered a hell of a lot. I needed to get back to the flat and think, talk things over with Liliad and decide what we wanted to do.

Stan noticed my change of mood but was enough of a gentleman to say nothing although he did keep casting querying looks in my direction; he merely turned the boat around and headed for the harbour.

As I stepped ashore, my thoughts tumbling in my mind like manic acrobats I said goodbye to Stan in a vague, pre-occupied manner but fortunately recovered myself in time to thank him with a genuine heart. He accepted my thanks graciously and we parted on good terms although slight bewilderment was evident in his expression.

Reaching the pub I went straight to my flat, hardly bothering to acknowledge Doug behind the bar or his dogs which were sprawled across the floor too lazy to do anything but wag their tails in greeting.

Liliad was sitting on the sofa where I'd left her, her gaze fixed on the chess board. I dropped down beside her and let out a deep sigh. 'The stranger's Philip Maccleson,' I said without preamble. 'I can't believe he was my mother's lover; it's incomprehensible an oaf like that but there's no-one else living in St Maabs who seems even likely to fit the bill. Most of the residents are too old or have been here for ever.'

Liliad looked at me, a question on her face.

I closed my eyes and laid my head on the sofa back. Thinking out loud I said, 'I suppose he might not always have been as unpleasant as he is now, it was over thirty years ago. He could have changed, perhaps something had happened to him to make him that way. Yes, that could be it; after all, we know he had a relationship with Tony Farquhar and *he's* such a lovely man he wouldn't take up with a brute, would he? Perhaps I'm being too hasty.'

I opened my eyes and was startled to see Liliad's sulphurous look. Her eyes, usually so clear and wide, their large black pupils drawing me in, were narrowed to vertical slits. I instinctively drew back expecting her to swipe me with claws.

'What? It's possible isn't it? Maybe I'll give it just one last push to find out for sure.'

Liliad returned her attention to the chess board. I followed her gaze. 'I don't remember those moves,' I said as I leant forward to examine the board more closely. My queen was caged in by Liliad's castle, bishop and knight. I couldn't immediately see any way out. 'Well, I can't play now; too much on my mind. I'll make some dinner.' I didn't look at Liliad as I walked toward the kitchen area. I didn't want to know what she thought.

CHAPTER 25

I knew from my hours of gazing out of the flat window that Philip Maccleson went out on Stan's boat Tuesday and Thursday mornings; tomorrow was Tuesday so I wasn't going to wait. I needed to put this thing to bed once and for all if I had any hope of salvaging my relationship with Liliad.

I told Doug I wasn't feeling well and asked to be excused the morning stocking up and lunch time shift. He was a bit put out but bowed to the inevitable when I claimed 'women's problems'. Quickly I dressed knowing that Doug was going to the general store first thing to stock up on loo rolls and hand wash so I left via the back door that led to an alleyway, thus avoiding the main shopping street.

It was still quite early, before nine so not many people were about. It would take me about three quarters of an hour to reach The Head so by that time Philip should be on Stan's boat and out to sea.

Walking the track were a few bird watchers but that was a good thing as I was less conspicuous, passing pleasantries with a few as we climbed. The track was wide enough for vehicles but you'd be mad to drive anything other than a 4x4 it was so rutted and potholed. I knew Philip drove a battered old Land Rover, I'd seen him in it when he came down to the quay. It troubled me a little that I hadn't seen it parked up by the cottage when I'd snooped around previously and yet there had definitely been someone in the cottage, they'd rapped on the window at me. Maybe I should have made *sure* Philip had gone out on Stan's boat. I was making silly errors; no wonder Liliad had so pointedly directed me to the chess game; tactics, strategy but most of all concentration and focus were paramount. I needed to get a grip.

Once up on The Head I detached myself from the bird watchers, veering off in the direction of the cottages. I quickly skirted around the perimeter checking that the Land Rover was gone and approaching the cottage from the side just in case I'd made a mistake and Philip was at home. Cautiously I looked again through the kitchen window. The breakfast remains I'd noticed before was now cleared away and, it could be my imagination but I felt the kitchen looked generally cleaner than it had. I then made my way over to what I now knew to be the sitting room window. Once again all was tidy and clean. Odd, but maybe Philip was the sort who only tidied up once in a blue moon.

Tentatively I tried the front door; no-one around St Maabs locked their doors except at night, something I'd found really perplexing when I'd first arrived.

The door resisted a little being slightly warped in the frame but with a low groan opened into the room. Nervously I stepped inside.

The air was scented with the smell of pine polish. The paperbacks on the bookshelf had been stacked properly, upright with their spines on display rather than the unruly piles I'd witnessed before. There was a freshly laundered cloth on the table and the armchair by the fire now sported a colourful throw hiding the worn leather of the seat. The fire wasn't lit but was laid ready.

I wasn't sure what I was looking for; something that would confirm for me that he was the Philip Maccleson from my mother's old firm. I needed to establish that before I approached him. I didn't want him to be in a position where he could deny everything, claim he'd never ever been in Dorset much less knew my mother and leave me not knowing for sure the truth of his assertions.

Looking round the room there didn't seem to be any-where one would keep personal papers; no sideboard or drawer unit. Things of that nature were unlikely to be kept in the kitchen so I made my way up the steep, narrow stairs to the bedrooms. There was a tiny landing, just big enough to turn around on with two doors off. The one to my right over the kitchen led into quite a large bathroom; at least it sported a sink and commode toilet but no bath – it had probably been a second bedroom when washing was done in the kitchen sink and the toilet was outside. There was a bucket full of water by the sink, presumably for washing. Why would anyone want to live like this? It was incomprehensible to me.

The room to my left was furnished with a double bed, chest of drawers and one bedside unit. A freestanding wardrobe was on the far wall and an ottoman positioned at the foot of the bed.

I opened the drawers in turn but they contained nothing but clothes as did the wardrobe. Shutting the wardrobe door I glanced up; I remembered as a child I'd kept my special, secret items hidden in a box up there but in this case there was nothing. I was dismayed – he must have some personal papers surely – everyone did!

I sat down on the ottoman – where next then realised I was sitting on it. I slid to the floor and kneeling, lifted the lid. Jackpot! Diaries, photograph albums, tax forms, receipts – all the paraphernalia of modern life. I settled down to browse.

Picking up one of the diaries at random I perused a few entries then, reminding myself to focus, I looked for those that covered the years he would have been at Bottomley & Farquhar assuming, of course, that he was *that* Philip Maccleson.

Piled carefully in date order these were near the bottom of the stack as one would expect it being over thirty years ago. I flicked through page after page and then Eureka! It was there in neat handwriting.

> *"Monday 6th June – my first day at Bottomley & Farquhar. Mr Bottomley a bit of an old woman but the other partner, a Tony Farquhar seems a nice guy. Hope this works out."*

A torrent of exhilaration ran through me, every nerve end tingling with excitement. It was him, it had to be, there wasn't anybody else. I sank back on my heels, picturing the Philip Maccleson I currently knew; surly, unsociable and reclusive yet the diary entries I'd read came from a much pleasanter seeming individual. They'd recorded outings with friends, holidays abroad, his architectural studies, promotions at work – there was nothing aggressive or obdurate in their tone.

I carefully returned the diaries in order and turned to the photograph albums. These ended some years previously but that wasn't surprising, few people kept albums these days; it was all digital.

Again I found the one covering the years my mother had been at Bottomley & Farquhar and there she was, all dolled up at the office Christmas party standing sandwiched between Mr Bottomley and Tony Farquhar, glasses raised in toast; all looking a little the worse for wear but beaming into the camera. There was one of Mary Jeffreys – she looked so young but then she'd told me she'd joined the firm straight from school and another of Philip and David Nigby, arms slung over each other's shoulders in friendly comradeship. I was totally absorbed, how long I'd been in the cottage had ceased to register.

Slowly I became aware of distant voices breaking into my thoughts. Quickly I stood, walking over to the window; it was some of the bird watching group making their way back down. I glanced at my watch; good grief, it was nearly noon. I returned to the ottoman replacing the albums with care and shutting the lid. Halfway down the stairs I froze; footsteps scrunched on the gravel outside as they approached the stepping stones that led to the front door.

I jumped the last four stairs and raced into the kitchen. There was no back door out of the cottage; I had only one option. Heaving myself up onto the draining board I opened the casement window, pushing it as wide as I could. Squeezing through I dropped onto the ground, turned and pushed it almost shut behind me, then crouched down below the windowsill, pressing myself as flat to the wall as I could just as the front door opened.

Footsteps on the kitchen flagstones came towards the window. I held my breath; there was a pause and then the window was pulled completely shut and the latch dropped. I waited, giving the person time to return to the sitting room and then made a run for it toward the other cottages, only stopping when I'd reached their far side.

My legs, giving way to nervous tension, trembled as I slowly sank to the ground. Leaning my back against the cottage wall I closed my eyes, trying to control the short, painful gasps of breath; it felt as though someone was standing on my chest preventing oxygen reaching my lungs. Silently I counted; one, two, three and on and on until the panic eased and my self- control returned.

I pushed to my feet intending to make my way back down to the village but as I rounded the corner of the building I caught sight of Philip Maccleson's Land Rover clambering up the steep track, lurching from side to side as it negotiated the rough terrain. I slunk back into the shadows; I needed to wait until he got inside his cottage before I made my escape then a thought struck me – if it was Philip Maccleson in the Land Rover who the hell was in his cottage?

Cautiously I circled the derelict cottages until I had a vantage point to Philip's front door. As he brought the Land Rover to a halt by the cottage side the front door opened. Tony Farquhar stood at the entrance, his hand held aloft in greeting as Philip stepped down from the vehicle. He walked across, a bag of groceries in each hand; it was the first time I'd seen him smile. Tony took one of the bags from him and as they entered the cottage laid a friendly hand on Philip's back.

I could hear, in the distance, the murmur of voices as a group of hikers came over the rise. Waiting until they drew near I tagged on behind and on their far side so they shielded me from any possible sightings from the cottage windows. They were a sociable crowd and recognised me from the pub but I found it hard to focus on their chatter. I needed space to think through all I'd discovered and decide my next move. Tactics and long term strategy needed to be considered and for that I needed Liliad.

CHAPTER 26

There was no point my trying to sneak in the back way of the pub as the only entrance to the stairs and my flat was behind the bar where Doug would undoubtedly be. As I entered by the front door Doug called across. 'Feeling better?'

'Yes thanks; I've just been for a short stroll; felt I needed the fresh air. I'm going to lay down for a while but I'm sure I'll be alright to do tonight's shift.'

Doug nodded in acknowledgement as he continued drying the beer mugs and restacking them on the shelves. I scurried up the stairs not wanting to be drawn into more conversation and eager to tell Liliad all I'd discovered.

She was still sitting on the sofa by the chess board but a little further back, her eyes closed as though she were dozing. I sat beside her, gently nudging her arm so as not to startle her. Her eyes opened slowly, a slight smile on her mouth as she registered that I was back.

I lifted her strings and we walked over to the window-sill. Making sure she was comfortable I lowered the top section of the sash window to let in some sea air. Then, taking the chair beside her I spread my hands out in front of me, splaying my fingers and rolling my head a fraction to release the tension that had built up in my neck. 'Well, Liliad, he's definitely the Philip Maccleson that worked at Bottomley & Farquhar when my mother was there. I found diaries and photographs that leave no doubt and, as if that wasn't enough, Tony Farquhar was there!'

Liliad's eyes widened in surprise.

'Yes, I know; I couldn't believe it either but it was definitely him. I'll have to try to find out how long he's been here and why. I'll just have to pray he doesn't come into the pub although he might not recognise me with my short dyed hair and change of name.' I paused, turning things over in my mind. 'Of course, I still don't know if Philip is my father; I'm going to need more definite proof. I can only hope Tony Farquhar doesn't stay long – he'll just be in the way. Sometime in the next few days I'll have a word with Margaret in the general store; she usually knows all the gossip.'

Leaving Liliad to mull over all I'd told her I made myself a sandwich and a cup of tea and settled on the sofa for a nap. I felt really tired; the morning had been more stressful than I'd anticipated and coupled with the walking up and down to The Head, I was physically drained.

◆

Early Thursday morning I popped along to the general store. Margaret had just received a delivery of dry goods and was busily pricing and shelving. I sidled up beside her, pretending to examine the items on the shelf.

'Hi, Vee; you OK?'

'Yes I'm fine thanks. Are these any good?' I picked up a packet of dried tomatoes.

'Excellent in casseroles; give a stronger flavour.'

'Really; I might give those a try sometime.' I placed the packet back on the shelf. 'Stan doesn't seem to have taken his boat out yet this morning; I thought he always took that Philip Maccleson out deep sea angling on Thursdays.'

Margaret straightened up from the bottom shelf with some difficulty. 'Yes, he does normally, I expect it's because his visitor's coming again today.'

'What, Stan's visitor?'

'No, Philip's. He came in the shop yesterday morning on his way up to The Head; bought some of that Bull's Blood wine Philip's so fond of; said it was his birthday.'

'Does he visit him often?'

Margaret shrugged, 'First time as far as I'm aware but then Philip's only been here about a year and I understand it's quite a long journey for him; comes from down on the south coast somewhere.'

'Wow that is a long trek. He's surely not staying up there is he? It's so …'

Margaret grinned. 'I know what you mean but no, he's got more sense; he's staying in Berwick and getting a taxi up here. Says he's going back home tomorrow so I expect Philip will be out with Stan again next Tuesday as usual. Anyway, why the interest?'

'Just curious; Philip's such an odd chap. I'd seen him down on the quay and he was really off-hand and then he came into the pub, just before closing time and was very rude to me. Since then he's been in the pub a few times; a bit more polite and I've tried to chat to him but he just closes down and goes to sit in the far corner but I can feel him looking at me all the time he's there – it's a bit disconcerting. I've mentioned it to Doug but he reckons he's harmless enough – just an oddball.'

Chuckling Margaret said, 'Well, it takes one to know one I suppose.'

'That's true. Anyway, better get back or my 'oddball' boss will be throwing a wobbly.'

That was a useful conversation; Tony would be gone by Friday leaving the way clear for me. I wouldn't rush;

I needed to get at least slightly acquainted with Philip however difficult that was and my best, indeed I felt my only chance, was to somehow engage him in conversation when he came into the pub.

◆

We were almost into September before I felt I'd made enough headway in my relationship with Philip to risk paying a visit to him in his cottage. We were hardly friends but on occasion I'd managed to get him to talk a little about his deep sea angling, life up on The Head and his fondness for the Bull's Blood wine which I found pretty unusual never having heard of it until I worked in the pub.

It hadn't escaped my notice that he was coming into the pub earlier than his original ten minutes before closing time habit. He'd have a few words with me at the bar and then retreat to a table in the far corner, near the door as though always ready to make a quick exit. None of this had passed by Doug and one night as we were clearing up he said, 'You seem to be having quite a positive effect on Philip Maccleson; he sometimes seems almost human.'

'I think he's just lonely and all that sour brusqueness is to cover up how shy he really is.'

Doug shrugged. 'Guess that's one interpretation. He certainly seems to have taken a shine to you.'

I wandered around, clearing a few more tables and stacking the dirty glasses on the bar. 'Why are the locals so against him? I felt like I was being warned off when I first mentioned him.'

Doug stopped wiping down the bar surface and turned to face me, the cleaning cloth still in his hand. 'I guess he just acted in a way that made people suspicious. He turned up out of the blue about a year ago having already bought the cottage up on The Head; moved in and made no effort to make friends with anyone and shrugged off people's warnings about the cliff erosion. Treating locals like they don't know what they're talking about isn't the way to win friends and influence people.'

'No, I guess not. OK, Doug I think that's everything.' I made a quick check around the room. 'I'm off to my bed.'

'Goodnight, Vee.'

As I lay in bed I made my plans for the following Monday evening.

◆

I knew I could buy the Bull's Blood wine in the general store but that would have pricked Margaret's interest and led to awkward questions so, when Doug was out in the morning, I sneaked down to the cellar and purloined a couple of bottles from his stock. It was risky as he didn't hold that many Philip being the only person that drank it but I didn't feel there was much option.

Unless I was very unlucky I figured Philip would be at home in the evening as Doug had told me, somewhat tongue in cheek, that he didn't come into the pub on a Monday night. 'Presumably because you're not there.' He grinned as he handed me my wages.

'I shall treat that remark with the contempt it deserves,' I said as I flounced theatrically out of the room.

The climb to The Head that evening was hard going carrying, as I was, the two bottles of wine and all the way up I was saying a silent prayer that Philip would be there. The Land Rover parked outside was a welcome sight; I paused giving myself a few moments to bolster my resolve and then went up and knocked on the door.

It was a few moments before I heard the heavy tread of feet on the stairs and the door opened. Philip looked as though he'd just clambered out of bed; his mop of thick black hair was dishevelled and his eyes seemed bleary, his skin sallow but maybe that was the low evening light.

He said nothing, simply stared as though unable to believe his eyes until the silence became so oppressive I held up the bag containing the wine and said chirpily, 'Happy *very* belated birthday!' as the bottles clinked in unison. 'Well, aren't you going to invite me in; it's quite a climb up here especially carrying these.'

Obediently Philip stood to one side as I sidled past him into the sitting room. He still said nothing so I kept up the bonhomie. 'Would you get us a couple of glasses and a bottle opener please?' I took the bottles out of the bag and placed them on the table. 'Your drink of choice, I believe.'

Philip turned and walked into the kitchen, returning with two glasses and an opener which he laid on the table before going to sit in the armchair by the fire as though the effort had all been too much.

'I'll pour then, shall I?' I said as I opened a bottle.

Handing Philip a glass I sat on one of the two dining chairs by the table. 'Well, cheers and once again, happy very belated birthday.' I raised my glass toward him and waited. For what felt like a lifetime he sat completely still, staring at the glass of wine he was holding as though he expected it to disappear as suddenly as it had arrived, before slowly turning his head to look at me.

'Why are you here?' he asked, his voice rasping, a croak of barely suppressed annoyance.

I sighed and laid my glass on the table. 'Look, I'm sorry if I've overstepped the mark but I heard it was your birthday a few days ago and thought you might like some more company now that your friend has left.'

Anger flashed in his eyes. 'How do you know about my visitor?'

'Margaret in the general store told me.' He glared. 'Oh, c'mon; you must know there are very few secrets in a community like this. Anyone new is bound to cause interest.'

'There are lots of new people here during the summer why should *my* visitor stand out?'

I raised my eyebrows in disbelief. 'Well, I'll leave you to figure that out; you're the mysterious one, living up here all on your own, not mixing in or making friends with people. I guess you're a curiosity.'

Huffing he asked, 'And my birthday? How did anyone know that?'

'I understand you can thank your visitor; he apparently told Margaret.' We sat in silence for a few minutes until I held up my glass again. 'Look, just have a drink with me to show no hard feelings. I *was* only trying to be nice.'

After a few seconds thought he raised his glass towards me and somewhat reluctantly said, 'Well, I guess you're here now and it is a hard climb. Cheers,' and took a large swig.

Relief washed over me as I took a sip; it was the first time I'd drunk this wine and I was pleased to discover that it wasn't bad.

Taking the tiniest sips – it wasn't my intention to get drunk – I let my eyes wander about the room. 'Oh, you've got a chess set; do you play?' The set was still in its box on the bottom shelf of the bookcase; I hadn't noticed it when I'd snooped around previously.

'Yes, I play – do you?'

'I used to but I haven't had a game in ages, I'm probably a bit rusty.'

Hesitating as he tried to come to a decision Philip eventually asked, 'Would you like a game?'

'Oh, I don't … yes, why not?'

Philip levered himself out of the armchair and slouched across the room. Collecting the box he laid his glass and the box on the table, indicating I should move to sit on the far side, my back to the window. I watched as he took out the pieces and arranged them on the board, his touch almost reverential.

'It's a lovely set,' I remarked as I admired the pieces.

'It was a gift,' he looked up, meeting my eyes, 'for my birthday.' There was a very slight lift to the corners of his mouth; about as close as he got to a smile.

I refilled his glass and we sat in silence, concentrating on our respective moves. I was careful to keep lifting my glass to my lips so I appeared to be keeping pace with his drinking but only took very tiny sips. Philip, on the other hand, was taking a large gulp after every move in an absent-minded kind of way, like a reflex action.

I'd noticed in the pub that he could knock it back but because he was invariably driving only ever had one. I just had to pray he wasn't the sort upon whom alcohol had little or no effect.

We'd been playing for about one and a half hours and we, or rather Philip, had got through one bottle of wine and was half way down the second when I allowed him to get me into a situation in the game where any move I made would lead to a serious disadvantage on my part yet this fact didn't seem to register with him. He shuffled slightly on the hard dining chair and reaching forward to move his knight his hand started to tremble uncontrollably and he slumped forward onto the table.

I hurried round to his side and helping him up managed to guide him into the armchair. He was as floppy as a rag doll; barely conscious.

Without wasting time I retrieved the bag in which I'd brought the wine from under the table and extracted the DNA testing kit that I'd ordered over the internet. Carefully I extracted two swabs. Returning to the now prone Philip I easily pulled his slack jaw down and inserted a swab, firmly rubbing it over the inside of his left cheek at least twenty times as directed in the instructions. I then repeated the process with the second swab, flicking both in the air for a minimum of fifteen seconds to dry. Placing both in the sample envelope I packed it all away again and made my exit, quietly closing the front door behind me.

Nights were drawing in and I'd been at the cottage for at least three hours. My night vision isn't good and I found the walk back down to the village a frightening challenge but I'd been up and down this track so many times it, fortunately, was pretty familiar and I made it to the village without mishap.

As soon as I got into the flat I repeated the swabbing process on myself, filled out all the necessary forms, packed everything into the return envelope and immediately took it down to the post box. I should have the results in three working days.

CHAPTER 27

'It's him!' I shouted triumphantly as I waved the paper in front of Liliad. Flinging my arms wide in sheer exuberance I danced around the room before dropping onto the seat beside her.

Liliad's eyes, wide with disbelief, were transfixed on the paper. I calmed down enough to read the results out to her before clutching it to my breast like a beloved child. 'You don't have to say it, I know, I've got to calm down and take things slowly. Don't worry, I'm not going to be so stupid as to rush up and fling my arms around him and announce that I'm his long lost child. I realise it's going to come as a huge shock; he'll need time to come to terms with it but when he does … well, there are so many possibilities. We could set up home together, not up on The Head, down here in the village somewhere. It'd be much better for him as he gets older, I'd be there for him, maybe get him to socialise more. I do feel he's already coming out of his shell a little with me although I don't think he'll ever be a truly social animal but then, that's how alike we are, isn't it; I'm not one for large gatherings or lots of friends either. Then there's the chess; it explains my natural aptitude for the game; I must have got it from him as Mr Theakston, the man I thought was my father, never played and Matt only ever showed me the rudiments; I was beating him when I was just nine years old.'

I paused for breath, barely able to control my excitement. I knew I was wittering on, Liliad's disdainful expression made that very plain and it was with some difficulty that I forced myself down from the high I was feeling to more practical matters.

I would have to choose my moment carefully, there was no point rushing things. I felt I needed to be on closer terms with Philip than I currently was. My visit to his cottage and our chess game had thinned the ice a little but we were still a long way from being friends. Instinctively I realised that if he was going to accept me into his life he needed to have formed some kind of attachment to me, however tenuous, first. Somehow I had to win his approbation.

Over the next three weeks he came into the pub several times staying for longer and all the time observing me from under hooded lids. I got him to tell me more about his trips out to sea with Stan; whether he was much of a cook (it turned out he was which was something else I must have inherited from him as my 'father' couldn't boil the proverbial egg and my mother was more a microwave meal or dining out aficionado).

Studying his face I could now find similarities between us, my dark brown hair a mix of my mother's light locks and his black pelt; his eyes, green with flecks of amber as were my own.

We were now well into September and the crowds of tourists had thinned out considerably making the evenings much quieter, giving me some time to come out from behind the bar and socialise.

One particularly quiet night I wandered over to where he was sitting. 'May I join you for a while, my feet are killing me?'

He nodded. 'Why don't you get yourself a drink?' He handed some coins across. I smiled my thanks and walked back to the bar returning with a G and T.

I said as I sat down. 'It's nice to see you in here more often. I know from my own experience that it takes a while to settle in, to be accepted by the locals.'

'I'm not sure that will ever be the case with me.'

I smiled a little sadly. 'The effort does have to come from you as well.'

'Is that a criticism?'

I shrugged. 'Just saying.'

We sat in silence for a while both deep in our own thoughts when he suddenly said, the words tumbling over themselves in his effort to get them out, 'Would you like … I mean, would you be willing … another game of chess some night?'

I looked up, meeting his stare full on. 'Yes, I would. Thank you. It'll have to be a Monday; I'm still working here all the other nights until Doug decides differently.'

'Monday's fine with me.'

Just at that moment one of the regulars approached the bar. 'Whoops, better get serving,' I said, 'see you Monday.'

◆

Liliad had been unusually quiet since the DNA test results had arrived; almost sullen in fact. I couldn't understand her attitude and challenged her one afternoon. 'I thought you'd have been pleased for me; I've wanted this ever since Inspector Munroe dropped his bombshell. I don't see why you're so against it; it won't make any difference to our relationship, you'll always be with me whatever else happens. I promise.'

Her response was an icy stare that made no concession. I sighed and turned away. I'd come so far, I wasn't going to stop now.

Monday evening arrived and I trekked once more up the track to The Head. It was only seven o'clock but it was already dusk. I'd thought to bring a torch for my return journey but actually hoped Philip wouldn't drink too much and be able to give me a lift back.

He was obviously waiting for me, opening the door as I put my foot on the first stepping stone of the path. He was tidier than before when I'd turned up unexpectedly and smelt of a pleasant citrus aftershave. It was clear he'd made an effort.

Taking my coat from me and hanging it on the back of the door he ushered me into the sitting room. A welcoming fire was crackling in the grate, the chess board laid out ready on the table with a couple of glasses of red wine and a plate of savoury biscuits and cheese alongside. Once again I settled myself with my back to the window.

'This looks inviting,' I said appreciatively.

He smiled, 'You make the first move ... to make up for my dropping off last time you were here, for which I apologise.'

I returned his smile, 'No need,' I said as I made my pawn's opening gambit.

We played in silence, the quiet only disturbed by the sparking of logs in the fire and the occasional crunch of biscuits. After a while I casually asked, 'Have you always lived this way? Up north I mean.'

He shook his head. 'No, I'm from the south originally.'

'Really, so am I; Dorset, well Dorchester to be exact. Whereabouts were you?'

'Same sort of area strangely enough. What made you come all the way up here?'

I gave my stock answer of redundancy and wanting a change of pace and lifestyle.

'Well, St Maabs is certainly that, especially in winter.'

He rubbed a hand over his cheek and I noticed again his unhealthy looking pallor and the slight trembling that had started up in his hands. He made his move and then excused himself, claiming he needed to get something from the kitchen, his balance unsteady as he pushed back his chair and stood.

I checked my watch; it was nine thirty and pitch dark outside and I was beginning to feel anxious about the walk back down the track. The wind had increased since I'd been inside and a few spots of rain were spattering the window.

Philip re-entered the room carrying another bottle of wine. He seemed steadier than when he'd walked out. 'Let's finish the game another time,' he said as he came to stand beside me. 'Why don't you come and sit with me by the fire. Here, have another drink.' He thrust the bottle toward me.

I hesitated, torn between concern at getting home safely and wanting to tell Philip who I really was. It had been a month since I'd had the DNA results, the delay was killing me.

'OK, I'll stay a bit longer.' I moved over to the fire and sank down on the rug as Philip settled into the armchair, drinking steadily.

'What work did you used to do?'

'Architect.'

I feigned surprise. 'Really, what a coincidence; my mother worked for a firm of architects in Dorchester, Bottomley & Farquhar. Have you heard of them?'

I didn't miss the brief second of recognition flit across his face. 'Can't say as I have.'

'That's strange; I wouldn't have thought there were many architectural practices in that area especially all those years ago. Are you sure you've not heard of them? They're both unusual names.'

Somewhat sternly he said, 'I said no, I haven't. Why the interest?'

'I just wondered; making conversation that's all.'

Philip took another swig of wine, placed his glass on the hearth and in one fluid movement slid out of the low armchair and onto the rug beside me effectively pinning me between himself and the fire. He attempted to put his arm around me and nuzzle into my neck. I jerked away from him, revulsion making my skin crawl. This was my father! I hadn't expected this at all; how could he possibly have got such an idea?

'Oh c'mon, don't start playing the coy damsel now. We both know why you're here.'

He placed his other hand on my right shoulder and pushed me backwards onto the rug, then swiftly moved his body on top of me, his mouth searching for mine as I twisted my head from side to side to avoid him.

'What's the matter? I thought this was what you wanted?' I struggled under his weight, 'or does the lady prefer a bed; I can accommodate that. 'So saying he levered himself up slightly giving me enough free space to bring my knee up, hard into his crotch. He yelled in pain and anger as I pushed him away from me and struggled to my feet, glaring down at him.

'You bitch!' he spat, his hands cupped to his crotch, 'what the fuck do you think you're doing, leading me on all these weeks.'

'I wasn't leading you on – not like that.'

'What do you mean, 'not like that', what the bloody hell was it like then?' He hauled himself to his feet, taking a couple of painful steps and dropping into the armchair.

I turned to face him. This was all going wrong, it wasn't as I'd imagined it would be at all. I took a deep breath, determined to regain control of the situation. Quietly I said, 'Brenda Theakston was my mother,'

'Who?'

'Brenda Theakston. She worked at Bottomley & Farquhar. She was Mr Bottomley's PA thirty two years ago.'

I stood, watching the memories flit across his face as realisation slowly dawned but he said nothing, simply stared at me.

'I know you worked for Bottomley & Farquhar so there's no point denying it. You had an affair with her, with my mother, didn't you?'

'No, I didn't.'

Angered by his denial I struggled to keep calm. Tersely I said, 'Yes you did and I'm the result – *you're my father.*'

'Rubbish!'

'But you *are.*' I ran to my coat that was hanging on the back of the front door and rummaged in the pocket. Hurrying back to the room I threw the DNA results into his lap. He sat quite still for a few moments before calmly picking up the paper and reading. 'How did you get my DNA?'

Defiantly I replied, 'The last time I was here; you passed out. I took a cheek swab while you were unconscious.'

'I see.' The coldness in his eyes as he appraised me chilled me to the core. 'So what were you expecting? That you'd make this revelation and I'd be so overcome with gratitude and emotion that we'd play happy families together ever after.'

A knot tightened in my gut. I said nothing. He gave me a cynical smile, 'I did *not* have an affair with your mother.'

'Yes you did; DNA results don't lie.'

His face contorted with a self-congratulatory smirk. 'I didn't say the results were wrong; I said I didn't have an *affair* with your mother.'

I hesitated; something cold was crawling over my skin as possible options flitted across my mind.

Philip paused for effect. 'I *raped* her.'

He waited to let his words sink in. 'It was after one of our Christmas parties. I offered to drive her home and the stupid bitch accepted. I must say, she was barely worth the effort.' He sneered in derision.

Our eyes locked as I digested the full import of his words. 'I don't believe you. If you raped her why didn't she report you?'

'Ah, now that's where I was really clever.' He settled himself back in the chair as if he was telling me a bedtime story. 'Everyone in the office knew she and old George Bottomley were very fond of one another and there'd been rumours, suspicions about their relationship for a long while; often going out for lunch, drinks after work, their obvious affection for one another. I told her it would be so easy to confirm everyone's suspicions; all I had to do was say I'd caught the two of them at it in the office and I'd make sure Mrs Bottomley knew about it too – in essence I'd ruin the old goat's marriage and reputation. Her loyalty was pathetic; she was more worried about him than her own marriage. It was Bottomley she wanted to protect. He was like a father to her.'

He paused again, eyeing me with clinical interest. My blood pounded in my ears as I tried to process all he'd said. Instinctively I withdrew a couple of paces, trying to distance myself from him. My initial shock and disbelief was rapidly turning to anger at the futility of my search. Liliad had been right, I'd been on a fool's errand from the start.

With a smug smile he continued. 'So you see, you're nothing more than an unwanted by-product conceived in lust on my part and, I confess, pure revulsion on your mother's. Why on *earth* would I want you in my life? You're *nothing* to me so just *get out* and take your DNA results with you. It'll help remind you of just how little you're valued.' So saying, he slung the paper at my feet.

Shocked to my core I could do nothing but obediently pick it up, turn my back on him, collect my coat and walk out into the night.

◆

I stumbled in the dark for about twenty five metres, my torch barely picking out my way; its beam smothered by what was now torrential rain being blown horizontally by the fierce gale. I could hear the sea below smashing into the cliff with a demonic force that frightened me.

A brief lull and then the wind slammed into me anew. Knocked sideways, my feet rolling from under me on the loose stones of the track I was petrified. I stayed low, huddling down against the onslaught. I dare not continue down to the village, my only choice was to retrace my steps back up to the abandoned cottages.

I struggled to my feet and keeping my head bowed laboured back up the slope. Reaching the front door of the first cottage I was in the lee of the buildings and for the first time appreciated the cleverness of building these properties with their backs to the sea. I pushed hard against the door's resistance falling in when it suddenly gave way. I banged it shut behind me and staggered across the room. Dropping down on the floor I propped myself against the back wall, pulled my coat tighter around me, closed my eyes and gave myself up to the anger that engulfed me.

I wasn't aware of the passing of time but eventually my mind cleared, anger replaced by a cold, calculated decision. Philip's confession, if you could call his sneering revelation a confession, explained a lot about my relationship with my mother. Briefly I wondered why she hadn't aborted me but then I realised, of course, she was a Catholic albeit a somewhat lapsed one but I guess destroying a life was one sin she just couldn't bring herself to commit. Ironic really, when the way she treated me effectively destroyed the person I might have been. Philip was right; I was of little value to anyone.

Slowly and somewhat stiffly I dragged myself to my feet, opened the door and stepped outside. The weather had eased and although it was still quite dark an exceptionally bright moon cast a frigid pale light, just enough so that I could make my way without my torch. I easily picked out the dark shape of Philip's Land Rover. I moved over to the vehicle and quietly opened the rear door. Just as I'd hoped a coil of rope was slung on a hook near the back (no self-respecting Land Rover driver ever went anywhere without a tow rope to hand). Placing the rope over my shoulder I approached the cottage. The light was still on in Philip's sitting room. I peered in; he was still slumped in the armchair where I'd left him, deep in sleep or more likely passed out from all the wine he'd consumed.

I opened the door quietly and entered the kitchen. When Philip had got up from the chess game he'd said he needed to get something from the kitchen. I was damn sure that wasn't just the bottle of wine; his slight trembling had stopped when he'd returned. I could tell there was something not quite right about him. The yellowish pallor of his skin, the bouts of slight trembling and an appearance of general weakness all indicated a health issue. As noiselessly as I could I began opening drawers and cupboards but found nothing helpful until I spotted the noticeboard above the drainer, a prescription pinned to it. It was for liquid morphine, only ever prescribed for intolerable pain due to its addictive qualities. I realised there must be a bottle of it somewhere and renewed my search. Hidden behind a sauce bottle and jar of marmalade it was about three quarters full.

I carried it through to the sitting room. Philip was still comatose by the remains of the fire. Taking the rope I tied his arms to the wooden arms of the chair; wrapped it twice around his waist and the chair back and then tied his legs together. It wasn't easy, the rope was thicker than I would have liked, but he barely moved.

I returned to the kitchen and made myself a coffee which I took back to the sitting room, placed a couple more logs on the fire, there was no point me getting a chill and sat at the table and waited.

At six thirty in the morning Philip groaned, stirred and very slowly opened his eyes. His attention was first drawn to the fire; I could see he was puzzling over how it could still be alight before his gaze travelled in my direction. He started slightly, attempting to get up, his alarm and disbelief apparent as he surveyed his bonds.

'Good morning, Philip. I trust you've had a good sleep.'

'What the …?'

'Please, there's no need to be alarmed, I simply needed to ensure I had your full attention.'

He struggled against the rope but it was immediately clear that any attempt to extricate himself was futile.

'Please, Philip, you need to calm yourself; I know you're not well.' I held up the bottle of morphine. 'What is it, cancer?'

He stopped struggling and nodded, his eyes glazed with fear and pain.

'So what sort of cancer have you got? Lung, leukemia?'

'Pancreatic so you see there isn't much point in our building any father/daughter relationship.'

'Ah, I see; you were trying to protect me.'

I poured a glass of the Bull's Blood wine and opening the morphine bottle poured some into the glass. 'I appreciate your concern for my feelings, I really do and in return I'm going to help you.' I walked over to the fire taking the glass with me and held it out toward the flames. 'I'll just warm this a little; I wouldn't like it to chill your stomach.'

Philip's voice was barely above a whisper. 'What are you going to do?'

Ignoring his question I said, 'You know, I'm surprised that you've been drinking any alcohol whilst on morphine; you must have been advised against it surely.'

He gave a slight shrug and looked deep into the fire. 'The morphine eases the pain and the alcohol numbs my brain; it's my choice.'

I gave a sympathetic smile. 'I know that pancreatic cancer is excruciatingly painful so I'm going to do what any loving daughter would do for her father; I'm going to end your suffering.'

As I moved toward him Philip pressed himself into the back of the chair, twisting his head from side to side in an endeavour to stop me but it was no use. I knelt on his lap, ignoring his gasp of pain as my knees dug into his thighs. I gripped his nose shut so that he had no choice but to open his mouth and bit by bit I poured the morphine laced wine down his throat. It all took some time to finish off both the bottle of wine and morphine as I had to take a break between administering each glass; it was surprisingly hard work but eventually it was done, Philip's laboured breathing evidence of his drugged state.

I sat and waited, I've no idea how long but I needed to be sure he was dead; I couldn't risk him surviving to tell the tale. Once I was sure I wiped down everything I'd touched, not only the items and furniture from my last two visits but also from when I'd sneaked in and found his diaries and photograph albums. Finally, I pressed his fingers onto the morphine and wine bottles and glass. It all took a long time but eventually I was satisfied all was in order. I untied his bonds and replaced the rope in the Land Rover.

I took one last disgusted look at my father and turned my back on him. As I walked down the track to the village I made plans for my future and by the time I arrived at the pub my mind was made up.

'You're late,' Doug said without annoyance.

'I know, I'm sorry, just fancied a walk before I started. Everything will be ready by the time you open.'

'Yep, I know that, 'Doug replied, 'you're a good worker.'

'Thanks for that; I'm glad someone values me,' I said as I made my way upstairs to remove my coat.

CHAPTER 28

By the end of September Doug was making overtures to me about going onto his permanent staff. I was flattered but it wasn't what I wanted for the future. I was thirty two years old and I wanted to bury the turmoil of the last few years and start again like a phoenix rising from the ashes.

I thanked Doug for his offer saying I'd happily fill in when he needed extra help but I wanted it to remain an informal cash in hand arrangement. He accepted this with good grace but apologetically pointed out that, in that case, I'd have to vacate the flat. I'd expected as much and had already been putting out feelers for other accommodation.

As luck would have it the old man known as Phil who sat in the pub each evening with his Guinness and newspaper had passed away a couple of weeks before and his small cottage was for rent at a very reasonable price, it needing serious updating and decorating. It was very tight but with the money I'd saved from my bar work and what I had left of my original savings I could just afford it until I'd established other means of income. It all went through smoothly and Liliad and I moved in during the first week of October.

By December I'd established myself as the 'go to' person for dressmaking and clothing alterations, (something I'd always enjoyed but had so little time for in the past). I helped out in the general store and café when needed and, as promised, behind the bar if Doug was pushed. I even did a few weeks in the pub kitchen when the woman who worked with her husband fell ill. All of this was cash in hand and I was making a reasonable income. I discovered a little bartering also came in handy agreeing to alter a couple of pairs of Stan's trousers in return for some of his fresh fish catch.

I was loving my new life; the variety and freedom coupled with a more energetic lifestyle resulted in me feeling better than I had in years.

Philip's body was eventually discovered three weeks before Christmas. No-one had bothered about not seeing him around; I'm not even sure that his absence registered with most people. Doug commented on it to me once but I just said I hadn't a clue and we left it at that. Even Stan wasn't concerned that he hadn't turned up for his last couple of fishing trips before they stopped for the winter. In the end it was his doctor from Berwick who alerted the police, concerned that he'd missed two of his appointments at the cancer clinic and knowing that he lived alone he'd raised the alarm.

It all caused a bit of excitement and gossip for a while but it soon died down and eventually the police investigation concluded it was either suicide or an accidental overdose, the latter supported by Margaret at the general store and Doug attesting to Philip's alcohol intake.

Christmas came and went and Liliad and I welcomed in the New Year with enthusiasm.

Snow had been falling steadily since Christmas and by the second week of January it was becoming obvious that soon the road between St Maabs and Berwick would become impassable. Taking my cue from the locals I bought a pair of lined wellies and stocked up on dry and tinned goods, filled my freezer and visited Mr O'Brien to place an order for a substantial delivery of logs.

Satisfied that I was as prepared as I could be, that evening I treated myself to a long soak in the bath. Stepping out I viewed my naked body in the full length mirror. The change in me over the past months was incredible. I no longer bothered with make-up; I'd let my hair grow and resume its natural colour and all the healthy eating and exercise (those climbs up to The Head) had built muscle tone so although my weight had only increased a little I looked far more solid than I'd ever done. I wrapped a robe around me and went into the downstairs room to sit with Liliad.

'At last we're truly home, Liliad. I've no need of any of my former aliases; Amelia Thompson, Joanne Simons, Coral Wright and most definitely not Annalee Theakston. I'm Veronica Maddox from now on!'

I wrapped an arm around her and Liliad leant in towards me as we both gazed into the flames of the open log fire. I let out a contented sigh. 'It's been a difficult few years but it's all worked out for the best. I just need you and my place in this community. You were right all along; I should have listened to you; I should *never* have searched for my biological father.'

I'd never told Liliad exactly what had happened that night on The Head, only that Philip had disowned me and I'd walked away but I think she guessed there was more to it than that but wisely didn't probe. Some things were best left well alone. We were happy, content, settled; there was no reason to think that would ever change.

By the last week in January ice had crusted on the impacted snow and even the pavements were treacherous. Negotiating the steep hill to the general store and pub was dangerous going down and even worse trying to get back up. Stupidly I'd run out of milk so, donning several layers of clothing, a woolly hat and my newly acquired boots I took my life in my hands and ventured out.

Sliding down towards the store I clung on to gate posts, door handles and anything else I could grab as my feet kept sliding from under me. Eventually I made the entrance and lurched in, almost smashing into Margaret's magazine stand.

'What on earth brings you out on a day like this?' Margaret asked in a tone that suggested she thought there were none as stupid as southerners.

'Run out of milk,' I said as I banged some of the snow from my boots. I was at the back of the shop, standing by the chiller cabinet trying to decide if maybe I should buy two bottles rather than one if the weather was going to get worse when the shop doorbell jangled. I turned to see who else had been as foolhardy as me. Shock caught the breath in my throat making a kind of hiccupping sound as I slammed my mouth shut and ducked behind the end shelf. An acid anger rose from my stomach to my throat as I listened intently, praying the newcomer wouldn't approach where I was standing.

Margaret was asked for some pipe tobacco and cleaners and turned to retrieve them off the shelf behind her. I heard the murmured voices of the transaction and then the door opening and closing once more. I walked slightly unsteadily up to the counter with my bottles of milk.

'Are you sure that's all you want? I wouldn't like you to risk your neck again tomorrow.' Margaret took the bottles from me and scanned them.

'Yes, that's all thanks. Who was that who just came in?'

'A police inspector from down south,' Margaret couldn't keep the edge of curiosity out of her voice, 'he's staying at Mrs Johnson's B & B for a few days.'

'It's a strange time to take a holiday.'

'Oh no, he's on official business apparently. Seems he's looking for someone and has been asking questions about Philip Maccleson. I told him I don't understand why anyone's interested; the local police and coroner were satisfied it was either suicide or accidental – either way I can't see the need for a bigwig from down south poking his nose in.'

My eyes widened in surprise.

'Of course, I didn't say *that* to him but it's what I thought.'

'So who is it he's looking for?'

'Some woman; he came up with a couple of names but I've not heard them before and the pictures he had didn't look like anyone I know either. I told him he was wasting his time; in a little place like St Maabs everyone knows everyone else.' She paused, thoughtful for a moment. 'He needs to be careful because he said he's planning on going up to Philip's cottage this afternoon. Can't think why; I told him there's nothing much there but I suppose he knows what he's doing. Going up there this time of the year, the weather can change in an instant and he's hardly dressed for it. Right, if you're sure that's all you want.'

'Yes thanks; I think I'll go home and hibernate.' I placed the milk in my bag and stepped out into the cold. The snow had eased for a while but the sky was still heavy with more to come. By the time I reached my little cottage my face was numb from the icy wind and my legs ached from the effort of keeping my balance on the slippery paths.

Liliad was cosy enough in her chair by the fire. I peeled off my outer layers of clothing and sat down beside her. 'Liliad, we have a problem; Inspector Munroe is here.'

The pupils of her eyes dilated becoming so large there was little colour left, my reflection a tiny doll trapped in a bottomless well. We sat in silence, each balancing our desire to remain in St Maabs with the potential threat that Inspector Munroe represented. The scales weighed heavily against leaving things to chance, on that we were agreed.

◆

Halfway through the afternoon I made a flask of coffee, packed some biscuits, a large carving knife and a screwdriver. Wrapping myself up in my warmest clothes I trudged up the track to The Head. I was gratified to see fresh tyre tracks in the snow; they weren't the right sort for any of the villagers' Land Rovers or 4x4's and it was obvious from the skid marks that the driver had had difficulty and the car wasn't the most suitable for these conditions.

From Philip's cottage windows one could only see the last few metres of the track. I knew I'd be very unlucky if Munroe happened to look out just as I was at that point but nonetheless I almost sprinted the final distance throwing myself behind the derelict cottages out of sight. Once again forcing the door of the first cottage I let myself in and settled down to wait.

By four o'clock it was completely dark outside and the wind had picked up considerably. I'd thought to bring my torch so wasn't completely blind. Stepping outside I crouched down and scurried over to Munroe's car. Keeping down below the windows I stabbed the screwdriver into a front tyre and listened to the satisfying hiss as it deflated. He wouldn't be going back to Mrs Johnson's B&B tonight.

Back in the abandoned cottage I helped myself to some coffee and biscuits as I listened to the wind increasing in strength as each hour passed. I regularly ventured outside to check Munroe was still inside the cottage, not that I thought he could go anywhere now that I'd disabled his car. Whatever was he doing in there? What did he hope to find?

Outside the noise of the sea was much louder and as I watched snow began to fall, lightly at first but increasing all the time. I hurried back inside and settled down for a long wait as blizzard conditions set in.

At eight o'clock there was a steady glow coming from Philip's sitting room window and I could smell wood smoke on the air. I waited some more, nine, ten o'clock. I was frozen by now and the promise of warmth in Philip's cottage won over against caution. I peeped through the sitting room window. Munroe was asleep in the fireside chair, his long legs stretched out by the fire and a kerosene lamp on the table giving out a yellowish glow.

Painstakingly slowly I eased the front door open, its creaking as it travelled over the wooden floor lost in the noise of the blizzard. Munroe grunted and moved a little but remained asleep. I undid my coat, sat at the table and laid the knife beside the chess set, still laid out as Philip and I had left it.

Another hour had passed when Munroe's head dropped at an awkward angle against the edge of the chair back his position eventually causing enough pain to penetrate his sleep and he began to wake; wriggling a little to ease his back and bringing his hand up to massage his neck, his eyes still half shut as he registered where he was.

'Nice of you to join me, Inspector.'

Munroe's shock at unexpectedly finding himself alone with me was obvious. In those initial waking seconds reality had stopped and his personal nightmare had begun. He made to lever himself out of the chair. I raised the knife a fraction off the table. 'Please stay where you are – although you could put another log on the fire; it's a little chilly in here.'

He stayed where he was, staring intently at me, confusion causing his voice to tremble slightly. 'Annalee Theakston?'

'My name is Veronica; Veronica Maddox; my friends call me Vee but you can call me Ms Maddox.'

Slowly gathering his thoughts Munroe said, 'No, I'll call you Miss Theakston because that's who you are.' He shuffled forward and obediently placed a couple of logs on the fire, watching as they slowly ignited.

'But that's exactly who I'm *not* as you were so at pains to point out.'

We sat in silence knowing that when we spoke the atmosphere would be a bruise between us of mutually inflicted pain. Eventually, his eyes on the carving knife, Munroe asked, 'What are you planning to do?'

'I just want to talk.'

'I have nothing I want to say to you.'

'No, but I have plenty I want to say to you. This game of cat and mouse that you've played with me for the past few years simply has to stop.'

Munroe shifted into a more upright position as though trying to create an air of authority. 'It will go on until you're locked up where you can do no more harm to society.'

I was affronted. 'But I'm no threat to society, ask the people of St Maabs. I'm well liked here; I help people out when I can, I'm friendly and pleasant. I don't pose a threat.'

Munroe sneered, 'You've posed a threat since you were a child.'

'Whatever makes you say that?'

'Dr Metcalfe; he told me that you'd killed your brother's fiancée, Addie Baxter; that's reason enough.'

'Oh please, Inspector, I was nine years old; how could I? Be reasonable.'

Munroe, looking slightly uncomfortable, backtracked a little. 'You may not have physically killed her but he said that you were definitely responsible for her death.'

'Was I, well, perhaps but I repeat, I was only a child with childish fears. All I could see was that Addie was taking my brother away from me – the only person in my life who'd ever shown me any love. I was jealous and scared. I didn't know she would drown, she was a strong swimmer, had won medals. I only meant to give her a fright. I was devastated at what had happened.'

Munroe stared at me, trying to determine whether I was telling the truth. 'But you didn't own up, did you? Even when your beloved brother was being accused.'

'You have a very selective memory, Inspector. I tried to 'own up' but you didn't let me; you had my mother remove me from the room when I tried to speak up in Matt's defence. You weren't interested in what a 'little girl with a wild imagination' had to say.'

Munroe squirmed a little in the chair. I could tell that he recalled his words but was still determined to excuse himself from any blame. 'You had plenty of time later to come forward, you could have confided in your parents.'

I snorted in derision, 'Oh, how little you know of my childhood reality. Talk to my parents? They barely acknowledged my existence. I was an inconvenience, surplus to requirements. I wouldn't have even had the *chance* to explain what I knew but in the end it didn't matter, did it? You found out how wrong you were about Matt's involvement all by yourself. What do they term it, irrefutable evidence coming to light?'

Munroe's eyes shifted away from me, his gaze directed somewhere over my left shoulder, as though that episode of the past was playing out on the wall behind me like an old movie.

I continued, 'My childhood actions *may* have contributed to Addie's death but I was only a child, a very frightened and lonely child but *you, you* were an adult intent on furthering your career; *you* wouldn't listen; *you* hounded Matt and wouldn't let up until, combined with his grief at losing Addie, it all became too much and he killed himself.'

Munroe wasn't going to let that go, his indignation evident in his voice. 'There was no evidence that was anything more than a tragic accident; that he stumbled over the cliff in the dark and, in any case, I'd already informed him and your parents of the results of our investigations; that it had become clear that he was innocent and that no charges would be brought.'

I shrugged. 'Too little too late, Inspector, *much* too late. My brother was a very sensitive person and the slur was there, out in the community. He couldn't face it. No, whatever slant you like to put on it – *you* were responsible for my brother's death just as much as you regard *me* responsible for Addie's.'

We were both silent, the air toxic with derision and disbelief.

'You've been wrong about so much, Inspector it amazes me that you've managed to climb the career ladder at all. Let's see now, you were wrong about Addie Baxter's death, you were wrong about Barry Mason accusing him of killing his father when he hadn't, you are wrong in your belief that I killed Melissa Hartnell and, although you have tried your hardest, you can't prove I killed your daughter. Quite a list, don't you think?'

Munroe clenched the wooden arms of the chair with such force his knuckles whitened, his anger barely under control. 'I may have made some mistakes but I am *not* wrong about you.'

I decided to change the focus. 'Tell me, Inspector, how did you come to believe I was in St Maabs?'

'It was from what I learnt from Barry Mason and then Philip Maccleson's death made me suspicious.'

I couldn't quite disguise an involuntary intake of breath at Barry's name.

'Oh yes, Miss Theakston; Barry survived the fire you set.'

I kept my expression bland. 'Another of your fantasies, Inspector?'

Munroe stared at me with contempt but deciding not to argue the point he continued. 'Barry didn't know you were here but he was only too happy to tell us what he did know; that you were making enquiries about a Tony Farquhar. I didn't think you'd be able to resist the revelation regarding your parentage and when we started digging, armed with Barry's description of your new self, it all fell into place. We realised you'd drawn a blank with Mr Farquhar and Mr Bottomley so only Philip Maccleson was left.'

'You mentioned Philip Maccleson's death; I imagine you consider me responsible for that as well.'

'It wouldn't surprise me.'

I raised my eyebrows in mock astonishment. 'But what possible reason could I have?'

Munroe declined to answer. Idly I picked up and moved one of the chess pieces, my queen. Glancing across at Munroe I asked, 'Do you play chess?'

He shook his head.

'A pity; you could learn a lot. It's a game of strategy and tactics; one has to think several moves ahead; try to anticipate one's opponent's moves.'

A loud crack startled us both as a knotted log on the fire exploded. I looked again at the chess board remembering my evenings with Philip Maccleson. 'Tell me, Inspector, do you know the meaning of Armageddon?'

Munroe shifted on his chair, uncomfortable under my scrutiny and wary of where the conversation was leading. 'Of course I do; it's the final battle between good and evil before the Day of Judgement.'

'Correct. It's also a term used in chess to denote a game guaranteed to produce a decisive result; to break a tie. That's what we're playing, Inspector; the Armageddon Game.'

Munroe let his eyes drift to the chess board then to the knife I held pointing toward him before looking directly at me. 'That's all it's ever been to you, isn't it ... a game?

You treat people like pawns on your bloody chess board. You're a psychopath and I intend to see you back in St Joseph's for the rest of your life.'

I eased myself upright, stretching and straightening my spine. Locking eyes with Munroe I kept perfectly still; a cobra waiting to strike. 'Since when have you become an expert in mental health, Inspector? I admit to having some psychopathic traits, for instance I like to orchestrate the show; it's fair to say I am self-assured, have above average intelligence and I confess to a certain lack of empathy but that is true of a lot of people – including you, Inspector.'

'How dare you compare me with you; I'm nothing like you.'

'But can't you see that you are? You don't consider yourself responsible for the way anything has turned out, do you? My brother's death is a case in point.'

Munroe focussed on the rug at his feet, his jaw set in defiance as his mind flitted over the events of the past. I continued as though patiently instructing a child.

'Just think for a moment; the majority of successful business people have similar traits. How often have we all heard the phrase, always expressed with a show of deep regret, "I had to let him go"? – a well-worn euphemism for "I fired him because my profit margin is more important than his livelihood and well-being." Not much empathy there is there? At least, not enough to curtail the "looking after number one" instinct.'

Munroe was incredulous. 'Are you saying you're not responsible for the things you've done?'

'Oh no, not at all … you misunderstand me. I've always known exactly what I was doing and my reasons behind everything.' I tapped my fingers on the table surface, pondering. 'Haven't you ever wondered *why* I killed Dr Metcalfe when I couldn't hope to get away with it?'

Munroe let his disgust of me show in his tone. 'You don't *need* a reason.'

I was annoyed. 'But I do, Inspector; I *always* do. Didn't you ever wonder why Dr Metcalfe was so keen to get me convicted and back into St Joseph's?'

'Hardly; you had killed his fiancée.'

'As I've said many times before, I hadn't but let's leave that for now. Didn't you at least wonder why Dr Metcalfe had gone to such lengths to keep me out of prison; to use my mental state as mitigation?'

Munroe gave a slight shrug. 'I assumed he simply felt that the psychiatric hospital was the best place for you; he was a well-respected doctor.'

'Oh, Inspector there's so much that you don't know. How did you ever get to be a DCI?'

Munroe's lips set into a thin line of fury at my insult but he said nothing.

'Let me enlighten you. I swear, on my brother's memory, that I did *not* kill Melissa Hartnell; Dr Metcalfe did.'

It was Munroe's turn to snort in derision. 'Oh really, Miss Theakston, what fairy tale is this?'

'The truth; Dr Metcalfe admitted it to me in that final therapy session. He deliberately helped place the blame on me as he wanted me back in St Joseph's so that he could, in his words, 'study me further'. I was his pet project, part of his research.'

Munroe scoffed, 'This is so far-fetched; you expect me to believe this?'

I sighed. 'I don't really care anymore.' I felt tired, I needed this over but Munroe wasn't finished.

'It doesn't alter the fact that you committed a murder.'

'But if a jury was given the facts I'm sure my actions would be regarded as just; an appropriate and deserved response to the situation I found myself in.'

'Don't try to sugar coat your deeds … the only thing that drives you is *revenge*!' He said nothing for a while, simply stared into the fire. I could tell he was reliving the events of the past few years. After a few moments, barely above a whisper he said, 'My daughter, Lily … that was revenge, wasn't it … revenge for what you believe was my part in your brother's death.'

I settled myself a little more comfortably onto the chair as a particularly violent gust slammed into the window behind me vibrating the glass and making us both jump. In the eerie silence that followed the waves could clearly be heard smashing into the cliff below as the gale grew in intensity.

Folding my hands I leant forward, my arms extended across the table top, the knife comfortable in my hand. 'Revenge is a very satisfying food, Inspector; it's no wonder that the God of the Old Testament liked to keep it to himself.'

'So that's why you killed Lily.' His realisation was tinged with the deepest sorrow.

I smiled, 'You don't *know* that I did.'

Munroe strained to keep some self-control. 'Of course I know.'

I looked down at my hands, swapping the knife from one to the other, splaying my fingers, stretching the tension out of them. 'No, Inspector you *do not know*; you simply *believe*. You have no evidence, no proof, all you have is blind faith like a religion and like all zealots you use that belief to justify your actions.'

Munroe glared at me. 'You did kill my daughter; nothing will ever convince me otherwise.'

'Obviously not but I repeat, you have *no* proof and yet you are determined to make me suffer for it nonetheless. Getting me convicted of murdering Melissa Hartnell was purely vindictive as once again you had no proof. You couldn't have because I *didn't* kill her. You are no better than what you accuse me of being are you, Inspector? Revenge is what you have sought these past years, pure and simple.'

'That's not true; I want justice not revenge.'

The knife still in my hand I made a mock bow. 'Oh, congratulations, Inspector, what a fine distinction but in truth 'justice' is no more than a sanitised version of revenge. It's a perception, not a universal value. It doesn't make you more righteous.'

My words hung, suspended in the air between us, arrowheads of truth caught in a photographic still. We were both silent as we contemplated them in our mind's eye; each weighing the validity of what I'd said.

I toyed with the carving knife, its blade pointing toward Munroe as it caught the reflection of red flame from the fire, as if it was already coated with blood.

'Do you know what I think, Inspector, I think you need to blame someone for your daughter's death simply to assuage your own guilt.'

'What? How dare you!'

'Yes, the more I think about it the more it makes sense. Lily couldn't wait to get away from you. She told me how she felt; that you suffocated her; that you tried to control her life, her friends. She went on that art course in Scotland to get *away* from you. In fact, your 'little princess' *hated* you. The special relationship you thought you had with your daughter was a sham.'

Furious, Munroe clenched his fist and brought it down on the arm of the chair, his wedding ring catching and causing the wood to ring out in protest. 'You know nothing about my relationship with my daughter; you view everything through the distorted lens of your own life.'

I smiled sympathetically. 'But I do know, Inspector; Lily and I were much closer than you think. She told me so much; how you used your position in the police force to carry out checks on her friends; how you wouldn't give her the freedom to "grow" as a young woman should; how you were so against her going away on that art course. It was control, Inspector – nothing more.'

A moment of doubt flickered across his face but was quickly dispelled. 'You're wrong; I wanted to protect her, that's all.'

'That's not what she saw … or Mrs Munroe for that matter. In fact, Mrs Munroe was your main adversary.'

Munroe's head jerked toward me. 'What do you mean?'

I shrugged nonchalantly. 'Simply that it was your wife who helped Lily break free of you; it had little to do with me. It was Mrs Munroe who helped encourage the relationship between Lily and Barry Mason; it was she who facilitated Lily and I resuming contact after I left St Joseph's that first time; it was your wife who financed

Lily's course in Scotland. I suppose, in one sense, you could blame your wife for Lily's death as easily as you can blame me.' I smiled sweetly. 'One thing's for certain, you won't blame yourself, will you?'

Munroe slumped back in the chair; a rag doll that had just had all the stuffing knocked out of it.

Outside the gale was reaching herculean strength, the crash of waves into the cliff face relentlessly clawing the land back into the sea. A scream seemed to hurl itself down the chimney as a sudden gust dislodged some of the stack dropping it heavily onto the roof.

I stood, keeping the knife pointed at Munroe. With supreme effort he raised his head toward me. His eyes were lifeless, his cheeks hollows that accentuated the bones of his jaw; the shrivelled head of a cadaver. For what was probably the first time in his life he was unsure; set adrift on a flimsy raft of self-doubt.

'The Armageddon Game, Inspector, remember – there must be a decisive finish. Goodbye, Inspector – it's been a pleasure.'

I hastily put on my coat, gathered up the chess set into its box and tucking it under my arm, hurried from the room. As I stepped outside the ground shuddered underneath me. Terror gave me speed as I raced away from the cliff edge cottage throwing myself into the lee of the three abandoned cottages that were a safe distance from the danger.

For a few seconds there was a break in the wind allowing an eerie silence to descend before a low rumbling built steadily louder. Fascinated I watched as in slow motion Philip's cottage slid elegantly closer to the edge as its foundations were ripped from under it. At that precise moment the front door opened. Munroe stood, silhouetted by the sickly, yellowish glow of the kerosene lamp; his head on that long, thin neck thrust forward into the night, searching for me. He took one step over the threshold just as, with a gut-wrenching groan the cottage and its garden fell hundreds of feet into the sea taking Munroe with it. A few seconds later, like a macabre comedy, his car slid silently after it.

Once more I pushed open the door of the first of the three cottages and collapsed inside. Closing my eyes I fell into a deep sleep of sheer exhaustion.

◆

I woke at first light. The storm had abated and deep snow lay in drifts covering everything in a mantle of powdered blue glass; a sheen of crystals. I was cold and my limbs ached; stiffly I struggled to my feet and looked around me. The cliff had receded by almost fifty metres and now the three abandoned cottages were unnervingly close to the edge.

I forced myself to walk toward where I knew, from familiarity, the track down to the village was buried. It was difficult but I managed to negotiate my way down sometimes sliding on my bottom as my feet went from under me. It was early and after such a violent night no-one had yet ventured out so that I made the sanctuary of my little cottage unseen.

Liliad was dozing by the remains of the fire but woke as I renewed it, putting on a couple of firelighters and some fresh logs. As the flames took hold I looked at Liliad and silently nodded. No words were required. We both knew that we were truly home at last.

I opened the box containing the chess set. 'Shall we play?'

Bibliography

LYNNE FOX spent her early years in Norfolk moving to Hertfordshire in 1975. Her first novel, Heads I Win, Tails You Lose, was meant as nothing more than a one-off personal challenge but having received several readers' requests a follow-up story, It's All in the Game, was written culminating in this, the final book in the trilogy, The Armageddon Game.

Lynne lives in the beautiful City of Trees, Welwyn Garden City, Hertfordshire.

www.ingramcontent.com/pod-product-compliance
Lightning Source LLC
Chambersburg PA
CBHW060756190726
48285CB00002B/453